Fatal Storm

Lee Driver

Full Moon Publishing

Library of Congress Control Number: 2011920914

ISBN 978-0-9846357-1-9

Published April 2011

Printed in the United States of America

Full Moon Publishing LLC
P.O. Box 408
Schererville, IN 46375

www.fullmoonpub.com

Praise for the Chase Dagger Series

"Lee Driver has written an exciting paranormal mystery that has excellent plotting, brilliant characterizations and an enthralling storyline."
— Midwest Book Review

"Lee Driver's Chase Dagger/Sara Morningsky series is one of the few truly dependable mystery series being published today. You always know what to expect with Driver: the unexpected."
— Craig Clarke, Top 1000 Reviewer

"The appeal of cross-genre novels is sometimes difficult to target, but this one should have no trouble attracting readers from either the mystery or the fantasy side of the fence."
— Booklist

"In Driver's novels it is impossible to separate the lure of the plot and the magnetism of the characters. The chance to catch a hell of a mystery and the growing, unfolding enigma of such characters as these is exceedingly rare. Don't miss the opportunity."
— Lisa DuMond, www.sfsite.com

"This is a delightfully nontraditional mystery that should appeal to a wide variety of readers. Let the series continue."
— Booklist

"The attendant breezy sex, violence, and action, coupled with bits of Indian lore and Einstein the talking macaw, should have readers clamoring for the projected next novel."
— Library Journal

Also by Lee Driver

Chase Dagger Series
Chasing Ghosts
The Unseen
Full Moon-Bloody Moon
The Good Die Twice

Short Stories
Sara Morningsky, *Mystery in Mind Anthology*
The Thirteenth Hole, *Mystery in Mind Anthology*

Written as S.D. Tooley

Sam Casey Series
What Lies Within
Echoes from the Grave
Restless Spirit
Nothing Else Matters
When the Dead Speak

Short Stories
Solving Life's Riddle, www.smashwords.com

For Middle School/Young Adult Readers

Remy and Roadkill Series
The Skull

*Some of the above titles are also available in large print,
audio and eBook formats*

Part One

Energy is neither created nor destroyed,
it just changes form

Albert Einstein
(1879-1955)

1 The storm kicked into high gear battering the glass dome with rain so loud it echoed through the cavernous foyer. A figure on the stairs halted as lights flickered in a continuous pulse, as though the house itself were alive. She waited, not realizing she had been holding her breath, and then the lights gave one last wavering flash.

"Great," she mumbled. Her fingers grappled for the railing as her foot cautiously sought the next stair. "It's just a little rain," she whispered, slowly working her way down the sweeping staircase. The foyer was the focal point of the house, reaching beyond the two stories to a glass dome. But the flashes of light played tricks on her eyes. Shadows appeared to linger on the second floor landing, jockeying for position at the railing to watch her careful descent. One minute she was contemplating how exquisite the aged mansion must have been during its heyday, the next she was imagining that every person who had ever lived here had just risen from the dust to watch her every move. She shivered at the thought and cursed herself for not checking the batteries in the flashlight.

A crash of thunder rumbled through the building like a never ending freight train. She could swear the entire staircase was vibrating. Lightning continued its spectacle, illuminating the foyer like headache-inducing strobe lights. Maybe it was the shadows or the flashes but for one sick moment she could swear the lightning was green.

She averted her gaze but the shadows downstairs looked just as menacing. She slapped the flashlight against her hand. How like her hosts to give her a flashlight with weak batteries. If she concentrated she could ignore the storm and focus on other sounds, like voices, heavy footsteps, or the clatter of equipment. Between the rumbles and clashes she should have heard something. Where was everyone? They should have stayed together, but it was her idea to go off on her own. The whole night had been boring until the storm. Then all hell broke loose. Were they hiding in a room waiting for her to run screaming into the night? She wouldn't give them the satisfaction. She was a Monroe, dammit, and Monroes never back down from a challenge. She squared her shoulders and forged on.

Her fingers cautiously touched the banister, far be it for her to clamp her whole hand onto the years of caked dirt she had seen on most of the surfaces in the house. As her foot contacted the next step, she felt something rush past—a breeze, a shadow, which stopped her cold. It was just her imagination playing tricks, she reminded herself. Had to be. Maybe someone had opened the front door. But then a cold breath touched her cheek, bringing with it a wall of frigid air.

Stop him.

"What?" She gasped and whipped her arm around but it didn't touch anything solid, only a cold that raised the hair on her arms. Her eyes peeled through the layers of darkness, and as the lightning flashed she could swear she saw a shadow next to her. "Deep breath," she told herself. "Stay calm."

The words came again, the breath cold and damp against her ear. When lightning flashed through the domed window, the shadow formed the shape of a man.

Stop him.

A scream caught in her throat. She tore down the staircase, losing her grip on the flashlight as it skipped and banged away from her grasp. She tried to remember the layout of the house. Was the library to the right or left? Did she leave her purse in the library or the living room? The thunder was so loud and continuous, she doubted the others heard the commotion in the foyer.

The floor came up quickly. Her feet touched a cylindrical object sending her sprawling onto the cold marble. *Damn, why did I have to wear my good leather slacks?* Heeled boots wasn't a smart choice of footwear, either. But she had wanted to look her best for the photographer who had taken pictures earlier. He was the smart one having left while there was still daylight.

She stole another glance at the domed window where the green sky turned in a dizzying circular pattern. Where was the lightning now when she needed it most? Which way was the entrance? She scrambled to her feet, embarrassed at her own show of fear. With arms outstretched to keep from plowing into a wall, she ran, expecting to reach the entryway but her toe struck something solid, a partial threshold or step. Her body crashed against a wall and then she was falling, too stunned to try to catch herself. She had visions of sailing down a flight of basement stairs and gave a quick assessment as to which part of her body she could afford to injure. Too quickly her head slammed against a hard surface. The lightning decided it had had a long enough break and commenced its macabre show, sending shadows darting and swimming in front of her eyes. But before she passed out Sheila could swear she wasn't alone.

2 "We should have brought out the candles before the storm started." Venus fumbled with the box of matches. The tip flared. She lit three pillar candles then froze. "Did you hear a scream?"

Josh straightened, tilted his head. Tufts of hair stood erect on the top of his head, his shadow creating devil's horns. Venus had to turn away because the flickering and dancing of the candlelight made the image too realistic. "I didn't hear anything. It's probably the wind. Let's get these candles to the library."

They moved quickly down the hallway, through the foyer and into the room to the right of the sweeping staircase. Venus kept her eyes straight ahead, avoiding the patches of dark surrounding them. Once in the library they located more candles and placed them on the tables and the fireplace mantle. Heavy velvet swags held the drapes open allowing the lightning to illuminate the room.

The storm had whipped into an angry frenzy, sending torrents of rain against the tall windows. The thunder and lightning display barely paused for a collective sigh before starting up again. The mansion seemed to amplify the sounds, sending them bouncing from one room to the next.

"Did you hear that?" Venus asked. A cry, faint at first, could barely be heard over nature's ruckus. It wasn't a scream this time, but a soft voice, a child's voice.

"Shhhhh." He ducked behind the tripod and peered through an infrared camera, the hair on his arms bristling as a bolt of lightning struck near the house.

"But you did hear it, right?" Venus gathered her long skirt around her as though it could shield her from whatever evil lurked in the house. She straightened and took a step forward. "What is your name?" she called out. "Tell us why you are crying." She had already tried contacting the girl when they were upstairs in the child's bedroom.

"Try again, Venus." The lanky man hovered over the camera while keeping one eye on the EVP recorder.

"Did you used to live here?" Venus shook her head and whispered, "I should have done a seance, Josh."

"Wait." Josh raised his head. "She said her name."

They cocked their heads, straining to hear. The storm was so loud it was a wonder they could concentrate. Venus tried again. "I'm sorry, honey. What did you say?"

The candles in the room flickered and swayed. Shadows darted around furniture and into corners, playing some weird game of hide and seek.

Julia

A squeal caught in Venus's throat. She tugged on Josh's sleeve. "Did you hear her say her name?"

Mommy?

"Oh lord," Josh moaned. "I hope our equipment is picking this up. Where is Miss Monroe? She should be witnessing this."

Lightning bolts flashed like fiery shards of glass, followed by rolling clashes of thunder. The sky outside had turned a repulsive shade of green with menacing dark clouds plowing across the landscape. Then the camera died along with the recorder.

"What the hell?" Josh flipped the on/off switch. "The battery backup went out on both." He raised the walkie-talkie to his lips but that wouldn't work either. "First the electricity, now the batteries? What's up with that?"

They heard a clattering of footsteps pounding down the staircase and into the library. "Hey. What the hell happened to the cameras and recorders?"

"Take off those silly glasses, Flea," Venus sniped. "You scared me half to death."

"I would have never made it down the stairs without the night vision goggles." Flea ripped the goggles off his face almost pulling his wire-rimmed glasses with them. "Boring as hell upstairs. Not a creature stirring."

"Well, we have some action down here," Josh said.

Venus rubbed her hands over the lit candles trying to add some warmth to her body. "I'm getting bad vibes from this house." As though in response, the lightning and thunder increased.

"You've been saying that since we pulled up in the van." Josh removed the battery pack from the camera and replaced it with a new one. He looked past Flea's shoulder. "Where's Blondie?"

Flea shrugged. "She went off on her own half an hour ago. Said she didn't need a babysitter."

"Well, everything's out again," Josh reported. "And this time we lost the batteries, too."

"I noticed that. You didn't recharge them."

"Like hell. I always charge them."

Josh looked at the chaos outside the windows. Horizontal rain bent the trees. Branches blew across the landscape, tumbling end over end. Through the flashes of light they could see a strange mist crawling across the lawn, rising up as though sniffing the air, then floating back down.

"Is there a tornado coming? We don't even have a radio to warn us." Venus checked the various pieces of equipment scattered around the table, most of which she didn't have a clue how they worked or what they did.

Josh motioned to Flea. "Grab a candle. Let's see if we can find Miss Monroe."

They moved in unison to the large foyer. Flea raised the candle and shouted, "BLONDIE."

Venus hung onto Josh's shirttail. "Don't leave me behind."

"What kind of professionals are we?" Josh looked at his two partners. "We have been doing this for two years. One thunderstorm and we're like a bunch of amateur teens sneaking into an abandoned house. We were hired to do a job so lets do it professionally."

"You're right," Flea said in agreement. "But I suggest we not separate."

A loud clang echoed near the front door causing even Josh to gasp in response. The three formed a tight cluster as they stumbled into the entryway. Near the front door a grandfather clock banged, its pendulum slowly keeping tempo.

"What the? How did...?" Flea stammered. "We were

told that thing hasn't worked in years." They watched and waited as it finished its tune and clanged three times. Venus could feel her heart clanging in time with the clock. Everyone remained rooted, not sure what was going to happen next.

Josh cleared his throat. "Why don't we check to see if her car is still here." They moved as though tethered together by a very short rope. Flea pulled the front door open, the wind almost wrestling the door from his grasp. The silver Jaguar was still parked in the circular drive.

"Now what?" Flea asked as he forced the door closed.

Venus pulled her phone from her pocket. "Anyone know her cell phone number?"

The two men exchanged looks. "You're the one she called," Flea told Josh.

"Yeah, but I only had her office number. Besides, the cell towers are out, too."

Venus studied the screen on her phone. "You're right. No service."

"Let's start upstairs." Josh steered them back to the staircase. "She was sucking down that wine pretty good. She's probably passed out in one of the bedrooms."

Outside the storm clouds gathered over the mansion, slowly circling. Lightning shot through the mass from different directions, looking for the tallest structures. Inside the mansion three people were unaware of the power that had gathered nor the danger they had barely escaped.

3 Simon set the stack of mail on Dagger's desk and motioned with his chin past the wall of windows.

The landscape was awash in vibrant fall colors. Trees were clinging to their leaves, unwilling to let last night's storm wrestle them from their branches. Dagger was walking the acres, a noticeable limp impeding his progress. The vegetable garden had already given up its bounty for the year. Sara had left him to his healing while she had prepared the garden for fall.

"He don't look so good."

Sara couldn't argue with that. But she was sure his problems were more mental than physical. Although the gun shot wound had miraculously healed, Dagger's ribs had taken longer to return to normal. "He gets stiff when he overdoes it."

Simon trailed her to the kitchen. "Still quiet. Too damn quiet. And when he does talk, he's short-tempered."

"He doesn't sleep well." Sara pulled cups from the cupboard and set them on the granite table. She opened the oven and checked the contents. "Can you stay for bacon and vegetable quiche? I don't think Eunie will mind. You look like you've lost a few pounds."

Simon pulled out a chair and hefted his bulk down, patting his stomach. "Yeah, my bulk isn't as bulky as before. Got coffee cake to wash down the quiche?"

"Will miniature cream puffs work?"

Simon smiled, the gleam in his eyes making them twinkle. He poured a cup of coffee while Sara made herself tea. "Tell me about the nightmares," Simon said.

Sara dipped her tea bag several times while contemplating exactly how much to tell Simon. The window over the sink let in a mild autumn breeze. Although temperatures were dipping into the fifties at night, they still hovered in the low seventies during the day. She tossed the tea bag into the garbage and took a seat at the table. Sara wanted to say, "If you had been through what we had been through, you'd understand why both of us are having nightmares." But Simon was aware of what happened in Nebraska after she and Dagger had found the city one mile below the surface. She had described everything in detail to both Simon and Skizzy during the long ride back after their two friends had arrived to drive their injured bodies home. And although she always referred to the injury as a gun shot, it was anything but a bullet that had blasted through the right side of Dagger's body. It was more like some futuristic ray gun that could have literally cut him in half.

"Sometimes his arms just flail as though fighting off intruders. But one night I ran into his room and found him sitting up in bed pointing a gun at his head." Sara took a sip of tea. Her stomach sickened every time she thought back to that night.

"I did what?" Dagger stood in the doorway, dark eyes shifting from Sara to Simon. Neither had heard him enter.

He looked more like a homeless man with his two-month-old beard, shoulder length hair, and stained tee shirt. Sara turned back to the table with a sigh.

"Maybe you should have hid all his weapons," Simon suggested. "And who the hell sleeps with a gun under his pillow?" Simon thought about that for a few seconds. "Then again, I forgot who we're dealing with."

"He hasn't been in any danger. I emptied the clip and the chamber that night and I've checked the gun every day since to make sure he didn't reload it."

"You've left me unarmed for how long?" Dagger grabbed a cup then yanked out a chair and plopped down.

"At least five weeks."

"Five...?" Dagger's glare did little to unsettle her. Sara took most of his complaints and grumblings with a grain of salt.

"Does he still have the nightmares?" Simon asked.

"Hey!" Dagger's cup hit the granite table, spilling drops of coffee. "HE is still in the room."

"Sometimes," Sara replied, ignoring Dagger. "But he calms down if I lie next to him."

Simon coughed out coffee at that remark while Dagger's face flushed red. Although Dagger suspected Sara had been in his bed by her scent left on the pillows, he had refrained from acknowledging it, more for fear she would stop. His laser stare warned Simon not to make anything out of it, but it didn't stop the sly grin from spreading across the postman's face.

"What's the problem?" Sara shot her own challenging stare at Simon. "The next time the gun could have been pointed at me. Why shouldn't I take all sharp objects away from him until he gets his head back on straight?"

"HEY! HE is still in the room. How many times do I have to repeat myself?"

"Still have your sunny disposition, I see. It's a wonder you have so few friends." Simon was one of the few in Dagger's tight inner circle and was the first to suspect Dagger of being more than just a stranger wandering through town. A lesser man would have shied away from even striking up a conversation with someone whose very stare could send the most vicious dog running in the opposite direction.

Dagger growled into his cup. "It's just the way I like it."

Sara ignored him and retreated to the laundry room.

"Don't even go there." Dagger knew Simon never missed an opportunity to insinuate more into Dagger's relationship with Sara.

"Not saying anything except to watch for the signs."

Dagger hated to ask him what he meant because it would drag him into a discussion he was trying to avoid. He let the silence stretch, but eventually his curiosity got the best of him. "What the hell are you talking about?"

"She's gone from being afraid of people, even you, to living and working with you, to shooting guns, fighting to the death to protect you, and you say she feels the same as you...that you are just business partners, nothing more. Well, when a touch turns into a caress and a hug into a kiss and her hand fits comfortably into yours, then that's a green light that shouldn't be ignored. Watch for the signs."

Sara returned and set a pan of soapy water in front of Dagger. He glared at the pan as if that alone would make it move. He still didn't say anything when she draped a towel across his shoulders and set a can of shaving cream and a straight-edge razor next to the pan. Only when she raised the blade did he grab her wrist and level a cold stare her way.

"I'm sick of your beard. You haven't shaved in almost two months."

"Whose face is it on? Do I tell you when you can and can't cut your hair?"

"Actually, yes. Need I remind you that the last time I went to the beauty shop for a trim, you barged into the salon thinking I was getting all of my hair cut off. It was a wonder you didn't come in with guns blazing."

Dagger's jaws snapped shut. Truth was, he loved her waist-length hair and was afraid Sheila, his former fiancee, had somehow convinced Sara to change her hair style. His fears were unfounded seeing that Sheila had little influence on his business partner.

"You do look a little like you just crawled out of a cave in Bora Bora," Simon remarked.

Sara handed Dagger an elastic band. Reluctantly he gathered his hair in a ponytail. Once done, Sara lathered Dagger's face and neck with shaving cream. Dagger winced as Sara pulled his chin up and took her first swipe at his throat. He held his breath for fear he would feel blood dripping down his neck.

"Maybe I should finish my rounds," Simon said with a grin, running a hand through his graying Afro.

"Don't." Dagger held his breath as Sara took a second swipe. "I may need someone to call nine-one-one." Sara was quick but that shouldn't have surprised Dagger. She always was good with a knife.

"The quiche should be done, Simon. Could you take it out of the oven?"

Simon hobbled over to the stove, grabbed the potholders and opened the oven door. "Umm um. Smells good." He pulled plates from the cabinet and forks from the drawer. "Can I have Dagger's piece if he doesn't survive?"

Sara wiped remnants of shaving cream from Dagger's face and smiled at the growing anger he displayed. She squirted aloe vera cream in the palm of her hands, then slowly ran her hands over his face and down his neck. He grabbed her wrists and pulled her hands away. It was difficult enough living and working in the same house with Sara, but the feel of her skin touching his was wearing down his self control. He ignored Simon's chuckle when he returned to the table.

"That's much better," Sara said, satisfied with her work. She carried the towel and pan to the laundry room.

Simon shoved a forkful of quiche into his mouth. "You are a far stronger man than me living and working with that sweet, young thing."

Dagger touched his face, wincing at the tender skin which hadn't seen sunlight in two months. It felt more like he had been sunburned, but the aloe was helping to remove the sting.

"Seen Skizzy lately?"

"Oh yeah. Has a new toy for you. It's a key chain gun. Shoots two .32-caliber rounds. Gets right through an airport X-ray machine because it looks like a car's remote."

"Really?"

Sara breezed back into the room, having caught the tale end of their conversation. "I read about those. Interpol reports they are made in Bulgaria."

"You're late to the game, Dagger. Gotta get back onboard." Simon pushed his plate away and stood.

Truth was Dagger didn't do as much Internet searches as his partner did. He hadn't spent much time with Skizzy much less done anything more than think about the underground city where he was raised, and BettaTec, a company he used to work for, a company that used to control and may still control him. That was what he wasn't sure of. His fingers instinctively reached behind his neck to a spot to the right of his ponytail. He felt the scar where part of a microchip was still imbedded, a chip that could no longer be detected because of the black cord necklace Sara's grandmother had given to him. She had wrapped the cord around copper wire, a guaranteed way to block any electronic detection.

"What you need is a case," Simon said.

"What I need is a fresh start."

"Thanks for the breakfast." Simon gave Sara a worried look as he turned and walked out.

4 Chief John Wozniak motioned to the distraught parents. "Please, have a seat. Can I get you anything? Coffee? Tea? Soda?"

The plump woman pressed a hankie to her mouth as she shook her head no. Leyton Monroe grabbed his wife's shoulders and gently planted her in a chair. Anna Monroe's eyes were red and puffy, and John was praying that his sergeant arrived soon because John never was good at consoling.

Another man elbowed the door shut. Sergeant Jerry Martinez, having witnessed the condition of the grieving mother, pressed a hot cup of tea into the woman's hands. "Please drink something, Missus Monroe." Anna smiled her thanks and choked back a sob.

"We don't have time for snacks and drinks," Leyton snarled. "My daughter is missing and the department is dragging its feet."

Chief Wozniak plopped one ample cheek on the edge of his desk while he waited for his detective to finish pampering his guests. You can take a man out of the seminary but you can never take the seminary out of the man. That was the reason people referred to Jerry as Padre. It worked just fine for John. Better Padre than him when it came to pampering.

"We are doing everything we can, Leyton," Wozniak assured him, although it was customary that adults be missing more than twenty-four hours before involving the police. Seeing that Leyton Monroe owned several newspapers and half the politicians in the country, the chief felt it best to cover his own ass by bending over backwards.

"And what exactly is this everything that you are doing?" Leyton shifted in his chair and eyed the two cops. His face was wide and his white hair fit like a helmet, as though it had to be stretched to accommodate the size of his head.

Padre sipped his tea and remained silent, letting Wozniak take control of the meeting. Truth was, they hadn't done much of anything, especially since they didn't know about Sheila's disappearance until ten minutes ago when Leyton and his wife stormed into headquarters.

"Don't you put out an amber alert?" Anna wailed from behind the hankie.

Padre tried not to laugh and could see John struggling to keep his lips from forming a smile. "Ma'am, although Sheila is your child, she is almost thirty years old. The amber alert is for children." Padre stressed the word children.

"Listen," Leyton huffed.

John held up both hands. "Let's hold it right there. Everyone take a deep breath." He went around the desk and sat down. On the desk was a yellow legal pad listing numerous questions spaced several lines apart. "Padre and I are personally handling this case."

"Well, that makes me feel better already." Leyton narrowed his eyes at them and folded his arms across his barrel chest. "I want the FBI called in."

"Leyton, please," Anna pleaded.

"Let's not waste anymore time." John tapped the point of his pen on the first question. "When is the last time you saw Sheila?"

"She packed a bag and left around four o'clock," Anna said.

"So you were expecting her to be gone?" Padre was puzzled. Sheila didn't live with her parents so how did Anna know what time she left?

"She called to tell me about the story she was working on," Anna clarified. "She was excited to participate."

John and Padre swung their gazes to Leyton. Their silence prompted him to fill in the blanks. He almost appeared to flush from embarrassment. "I was against her working the story but she insisted it was a hot topic."

"She's going to miss her salon appointment," Anna interjected.

"A haircut?" John's pen tapped several times on the notepad. "Maybe she rescheduled."

"Oh no. It's very hard to get in to see Enrique. He comes in from Chicago once a month and he is booked from seven in the morning until seven at night. Sheila and I have a standing appointment at eight o'clock." She ran a hand through her nest of curls, suddenly aware her hair must look a mess. "We're going to miss it," she sniffed.

Leyton wrapped a beefy arm around his wife. "I tried calling the outfit she was doing the story with, but all I got was their recorder."

"I've tried Sheila's cell phone. She isn't answering," Anna said between sniffles.

"What about her boyfriend?" John knew Sheila dated one of the homicide detectives. Her current squeeze was Joe Spagnola.

"She doesn't have any boyfriends." Leyton shot a glare at his wife, daring her to contradict him. Unless the boyfriend was a duke or an oil sheik, Leyton never acknowledged that his daughter was dating.

"Back to the story she was working on." Padre felt John had been away from interrogations for too long because he had forgotten the golden rule to take control of the interview.

"She was spending the night at that mansion with a ghost hunting group," Leyton said, his voice lowered to a whisper for fear he might be overheard by the officers in the outer office.

"Ghost hunting?" John's bushy eyebrows crawled up his forehead. Why would the *Daily Herald* be doing a story about ghosts? "What group is that?"

"That Indiana Paranormal Investigators were spending the night at the Sebold mansion. They were setting up cameras and filming anything and everything that moved. Sheila planned to spend the entire night there. I thought it was a waste of time and energy, but Sheila convinced me it was a hot topic for our magazine section and she had an ulterior motive. She wanted to debunk them." Leyton checked his watch. "She said they usually break down around five in the morning and the IPI group goes back to their bat caves to catch some sleep before going over their film. When Sheila didn't show to pick up her mother this morning, we got concerned. She usually comes early, around seven o'clock to have breakfast with Anna. I called the doorman at Sheila's building but he didn't see her come home. So we drove over and used our key to check her condo. She wasn't there."

"That mansion is on the east side of town, in an unincorporated area. Some parts of the area lost power last night so the storm might have knocked out a couple towers." John went back to his list of questions. "Give me her license plate number so I can see if we can track her car's location."

"HOTSTUF," Leyton replied, another blush rising on his cheeks. "What can I say? She's had that vanity plate since she was a teen."

Padre wrote the number down and walked out of the office.

"Any idea what she was wearing when she left yesterday?"

Leyton looked to his wife who shrugged. "She was going to go home and change into her grubbies first," Anna replied.

"Did you check out this group? Are they legitimate?"

"Sheila did," Leyton replied. "She showed me their web site, but I have to confess, I thought the whole story and what the group does is a bunch of hogwash."

John picked up his phone and punched the intercom. "Lou, run a check on," he checked the notes he had written, "Indiana Paranormal Investigators and call me ASAP."

Padre returned and announced, "Her car is on the east side of town, probably still parked at the mansion. I'll take a ride out there."

"I'll go with you." John shoved the notepad aside. The Monroes hadn't told him anything useful.

"I'm coming with you." Leyton stood and moved toward the door.

"Me too." Anna followed suit.

"Anna." Leyton struggled to adjust from irritation to concern. "I think it's best if you go home, dear. Sheila may call or stop by and no one will be home. You can call me on my cell if you hear from her."

John's intercom buzzed. He answered, not hearing anything worth writing down. "That's it? Run a background check, names, bios, addresses." Satisfied, he hung up and reported, "We don't have any complaints or reports on the IPI. They appear to be a reputable organization but I'm having the members checked out."

Leyton scoffed. "They may not have committed any felonies but an organization that searches for anything that goes bump in the night is hardly reputable."

5 Sheila woke with a start. She took a deep breath, letting her eyes adjust to the light. It took a few seconds for her to remember where she was and what had happened to her. Of course. The Sebold mansion. But why was she there? The last thing she remembered was walking down the staircase when the flashlight died, but then what? She raised herself up on one elbow, then groaned and touched a bump on the back of her head. The room started to spin and a wave of nausea forced her back down. She didn't remember being struck with anything. Perhaps she passed out and banged her head on the floor. Maybe she fell down the staircase. She vaguely remembered slipping on something, maybe the flashlight she had dropped. She gave her eyes a few minutes to stop spinning and focus. For one thing, this room was small, no larger than six hundred square feet. There were bookcases so it was probably a study or library but the library at the Sebold mansion was huge. Perhaps she passed out and someone carried her to another room. There were enough in the mansion to choose from.

She tried again, slowly this time, propping herself up on one elbow, waiting for the nausea to subside. The Persian area rug was plush and expensive. If it was one thing Sheila was an expert at it was recognizing what was real and what wasn't and this rug was the real thing. The brocade couch was shiny from wear but she didn't recall seeing this fabric at the mansion.

She carefully maneuvered her body to a sitting position. No snags in her angora sweater or stains on her black leather pants. She felt her neck. Her three hundred dollar silk scarf was gone. She checked her wrist. The thousand dollar watch was still there so she hadn't been robbed. However, her watch had stopped. She tapped it several times. The second hand didn't move. "Must need a battery." Her surroundings were sparse. An ornate lamp was on the end table and another on a writing desk. There were two leather high-backed chairs. If she had paid more attention to her mother's interior decorator she would know if the chairs were Queen Anne or Louie the Fourteenth.

She pushed herself to a standing position and tested her legs. So far so good but she wished she had a bottle of Tylenol about now. Shutters were folded back from the two windows but Sheila didn't remember any of the windows having shutters. The windows at the Sebold mansion had velvet drapes held back by swag ties. Not one window at the Sebold had shutters. Outside the sky was overcast, but the light hurt her eyes nonetheless.

A chill crept through her body as she looked out onto a field of wild flowers. One large oak tree in the yard had a tire swing hanging from a branch. The trees should be ripe with fall colors and the wild flowers should be nothing but yellow stalks. These leaves were a vibrant green and wild flowers stood strong and colorful. She moved cautiously to an adjoining room which was twice the size of the study. A dining room table was situated in the center of the room surrounded by ten ornate high-backed chairs. A large buffet rested against one wall, the glass doors protecting floral-print China. This dining room was large but still nowhere near the size of the Sebold dining room.

Sheila backed out of the room and stumbled her way into the foyer where a staircase led up to another floor. Where was her purse? Where were her keys? Thank god her Jaguar only required her thumbprint to start. She yanked open the door and stepped out onto a rickety wooden porch. Where was the brick veranda? A trench of mud surrounded the house. The rain had lessened to a slight drizzle, but where was the driveway? There weren't any cars. This was all wrong. There should be a street at the end of a long driveway and street lights. Instead, an aged barn listed in the distance, its foundation struggling to keep the remaining clapboards held together. She held onto the railing as she made her way along the porch to the corner of the house. Her boots clacked along the wood. Where were the oak benches? The overgrown hedges? She suddenly felt faint. She held onto the railing until the dizziness subsided. This definitely wasn't the Sebold mansion. She wasn't even sure she was still in Cedar Point, Indiana. She leaned against the post and sighed. "I think I just fell down a rabbit hole"

6 The three men stood on the circular drive and studied the mansion sprawled in front of them. It was a hulking two-story building of dark stone, sharp peaks and gargoyle-topped turrets fitting of a Stephen King novel. Shrubs of spiked thorns hugged the front of the mansion as though guarding it from intruders. Ominous couldn't even begin to describe the place. They had driven past the entrance twice unaware of what was beyond the tall evergreens and thick brush. The mansion was tucked in back of acres of overgrowth.

They made their way up the drive in silence, past the two vans with IPI printed on the sides. Leyton and Padre stopped to inspect Sheila's silver Jaguar. It was unlocked. Padre punched the button to unlock the trunk. Leyton took several steps back and let Chief Wozniak lift the trunk lid.

"Clear," Wozniak declared. He moved several cleaning towels aside as Leyton joined him. "Anything out of the ordinary, Leyton?"

"No," he replied with a sigh, almost sounding disappointed that they didn't find Sheila's body stuffed in the trunk.

Two patrol cars pulled up behind Wozniak's Buick and Leyton's Mercedes. Four officers from the Cedar Point police department emerged from each of the cars.

Wozniak held up a hand to signal them to halt. "Thought we could use some manpower to help in the search."

They trudged up the five stone steps to where three people huddled on an oak bench outside the front door. A uniformed state patrolman stood guard over the three. He was tall and thin but stood ramrod straight. Somewhere on his resume was a military background.

Padre could see Leyton prepare to pounce on the three so Wozniak stretched his arm out and blocked Leyton from advancing, but it didn't stop the distraught father from moving back and forth on the balls of his feet like some prize fighter waiting for the bell to ring. The chief introduced himself, Padre and Leyton.

"Sergeant Jack Jackson, sir. They called our department an hour ago. Our desk sergeant told them to leave all of their equipment and belongings in the house. We haven't touched anything since your call."

"Thanks. Is your commander sending anyone else to assist?"

"I'm the only person they could spare, but I see you brought help." Jackson nodded toward the two patrol cars.

"Where's my daughter?" Leyton yelled, pointing a finger beyond John's outstretched arm.

"Leyton," John cautioned. "You can stay only if you let me handle this. If you cause a disruption I will have you escorted back to Cedar Point. Is that clear?" Leyton Monroe's right eye twitched as he grimaced in anger. John repeated his order. "IS THAT CLEAR?"

"YES," Leyton snapped.

A cool breeze chased leaves across the stone veranda.

The sun struggled to burn its way through the overcast sky but the clouds were too stubborn and thick. Weather forecasters predicted more rain and severe storms for the next two days.

"Let's move this party inside." John motioned toward the door.

Padre studied the three as they stood. One Lurch, one geek and a flower child. How could they expect to be taken seriously? The flower child examined Leyton as though he were a fabric swatch.

"Your aura is very dark," she announced.

"What?" Leyton drew back and glared at her.

"Inside, now." John motioned everyone to move. He flashed an unspoken message at Padre.

A stale, musty odor rushed to greet them in the entryway. A grandfather clock loomed in the corner, frozen at three o'clock. Dark wood paneling and faint light made the entryway appear like an entrance into a tunnel, if it hadn't been for what lie beyond. A spacious room which might have been used as a receiving area had a staircase in the middle which swept up to a landing. From there it branched off in two directions. They craned their necks as though admiring the Sistine Chapel.

"I don't like this house," the flower child whispered.

John turned to the eight patrolmen trailing them. "Four of you start on the first floor. The rest of you hit the second. Look for signs of a struggle, blood, any personal belongings of Miss Monroe's. Don't touch anything. Just log what you see and report back. Got it?" They all nodded and separated into two groups.

John sequestered everyone in the library to the right of the staircase. The room was wall to wall bookcases with a stone fireplace against one wall and groupings of plush furniture dotting the floor. Various pieces of equipment littered a long conference table. On the wall by the fireplace was a family portrait. The man and woman were seated on a couch, one of her hands rested on his arm. Her other arm was wrapped around a toddler seated on her lap. The child was around two years of age. Her eyes were bright and her hair strawberry blonde. The father had a scar just above his right eye.

"The Sebold family, I presume?" Chief Wozniak said.

"Very wealthy and very cursed," the flower child said with a shiver.

The chief pulled Padre aside and said, "Usually we would question these three separately, but I don't want them out of my sight."

"Agreed. How do you want to handle it?"

"You start the questioning. I'll jump in from time to time. Start with whoever the hell the leader is. I'd say the tall one."

John motioned Jack over. "I told my men just to do a quick walk through the house. When they are through, have them search the property, two in each direction. There are walkie-talkies in the cars. Have them contact me if they find anything out of the ordinary. They have a photo of the missing person." He waited for the sergeant to leave, then turned back to the group. Leyton stood over them like the hulking gargoyle on the roof's turret.

"Mister Monroe is Sheila's father," John started. "He is here to listen and learn but not to interfere. Isn't that right, Leyton?"

Leyton turned his wrath on the chief, but after a few seconds snorted his agreement and reluctantly sat down on one of the high back throne chairs. John pushed a button on the recorder, then nodded toward Padre who pulled out several sheets of paper.

"Josh McReady?"

"That's me," Lurch replied. His hair was as red as the chief's. Macabre tattoos of skulls and snakes covered his arms. He looked more like an overgrown kid in sagging cutoffs and a tee shirt with a skull and cross bones in the center.

"You founded the Indiana Paranormal Investigators two years ago. Is that correct?"

"Yes, me and Flea, I mean Curt Fleeter."

"That's me." The geek gave a limp wave but dropped his hand quickly when he saw the scowl forming on Leyton's face. The thick glasses made his eyes resemble a cartoon character's. "I handle the electronic equipment although we are both fairly knowledgeable about electronics. Me, of course, more than Josh," he added.

Padre turned toward the flower child. "Veronica Ernstine."

"I go by Venus now," she replied. "Just my first name."

"Oh jezzus." Leyton gave an eye roll toward the ceiling but stared in amazement as though impressed with the wood moulding.

"You met Josh when you attended Northwestern University and..."

"For crissake," Leyton snapped. "Let's cut this bullshit and ask them what happened last night."

"Leyton," John cautioned. "We have to confirm their identity for the record, so please..."

"All right, okay." Leyton folded his arms across his chest.

"Move on," John said.

"What time did you arrive?"

Josh went through the timeline, how his trio had arrived at three o'clock to set up. Sheila didn't arrive until four-thirty. They had explained their equipment and procedure to Sheila as a photographer snapped numerous photos. "Her notes are still here." Josh motioned at the notebook at the end of the table. "We did a walk-through of the house before it got too dark. Then we ate and waited."

"Waited for what?" Padre asked.

"You know." Josh motioned with his hands. "For things to go bump in the night."

"And man did they ever," Flea said with the excitement of a four-year-old. Washed out jeans hung on his bony frame. His arms were in need of a gym as there appeared to be very little muscle mass under his shirt.

"Creeped me out," Venus said with a shiver.

John and Padre exchanged glances. Leyton had a permanent scowl on his face.

"When is the last time you saw Miss Monroe?" Padre asked.

"Around three this morning, or a little before three.

We were getting some really good EVP readings."

"EVP?" Padre asked.

"Electronic voice phenomenon. Usually what we can't hear is sometimes picked up by our EVP recorder. But last night was phenomenal," Josh added with a wide grin.

"Yeah," Flea agreed. "It was awesome. We caught it all on tape."

"I should have conducted a seance," Venus added with a sigh.

Leyton opened his mouth but John held up his hand to head him off.

"Anyway," Josh continued, "we were all on the second floor. Then Venus and I made our way to the first floor. We were looking for candles in the kitchen because we were losing power."

"And where was Miss Monroe at the time?" Padre asked.

"She went off on her own," Josh replied. "We each had flashlights and she wanted to, I don't know, check things out for herself."

"Why didn't you just turn the damn lights on?" Leyton snarled.

"You don't investigate haunted houses with lights on," Josh snapped.

"What? The light hurts their eyes?" Leyton rolled his eyes toward John.

"Besides, the power went out," Venus reminded them.

Padre suppressed a smile. "So then what happened?"

"When Josh and I returned to the library, we heard her," Venus offered.

"Miss Monroe?" Padre asked.

"No, the little girl."

"Little girl?" John asked.

"It was Julia," Venus clarified. "That's who went missing back in..."

"We don't need a history lesson."

"Leyton, if you don't mind." The chief was ready to send Leyton home. "Just let them finish."

"Our research identified the original owners of the house as Jonathan and Marian Sebold. Julia was the daughter." Venus started to add.

"Back to Sheila Monroe," Padre said.

"So, Venus and I were in the library, Flea was still upstairs, but Blondie..."

"She has a name, dammit," Leyton huffed.

"Uh, yes. Sorry. Sheila was god knew where," Josh replied.

"There was a terrible storm," Flea interjected. "We lost power, it like knocked out all of our electronics. We thought we heard a scream but it was only the wind howling. Must have been a tornado because, like man, I have never seen a storm that severe before. Anyway, we took candles and searched the entire house. We called out her name. None of our cell phones were working. The walkie-talkies were out so we waited in the ballroom for daylight."

"So you left her." It almost sounded as though Leyton's voice had cracked. "I'll sue the lot of you for neglect."

"Hey, her car was still parked outside so we knew she was still somewhere in the house," Josh argued. "Besides, she signed an agreement not to hold us accountable."

"And I have ten lawyers on staff who will drill holes in that agreement." Leyton's threat was interrupted by John's walkie-talkie.

"Go ahead, Jack"

"We have a body, Chief."

7

"Hey, big boy. How about a cheese curl?" Sara poked the treat between the grating in the door, but the scarlet macaw looked past her shoulder and trained one ringed eye on Dagger. "Come on Einstein. You like cheese curls." Without turning she said, "Dagger, you are making Einstein nervous. You pace like a caged animal. You've avoided playing with him, and he can tell something is wrong. You know he's very sensitive."

Dagger yanked open his desk drawer, pulled out a Brazil nut, and held it up. "His only problem is he doesn't recognize me without my beard. All he sees is razor burn." He shoved the Brazil nut through the grating and took time to rub the top of Einstein's head. The macaw grabbed the treat with one claw, studied it, squawked his approval, and flew to the top of the fifteen foot tree in his aviary.

"What you need is a case."

"What I need is food."

"I'll buy you lunch. Just listen to a few of these first." Sara sifted through the opened mail and pulled out a letter. Dagger Investigations was never advertised. People heard about them only through referrals. Dagger used a post office box which Simon checked and hand delivered the contents several times a week.

"Did you take your vitamins?"

"Yes, all eighty million of them. I feel like a walking chemical factory." Dagger plopped down on the couch and rested his legs on the coffee table.

"There aren't eighty million. Such a baby." Sara snapped the letter open. "Here's one. How about the case of the missing heirloom. A vase from the Ming Dynasty which has been in the family for fifty years disappeared while the family was in Europe."

"Inside job. Tell them to check a family member who needed drug money." Dagger stretched out, hands behind his head. "Could also be one of the cleaning people." He glanced up at the steel crosswalk which bisected the upper floor. The windows on the first floor extended all the way to the ceiling. Above the crosswalk was a large skylight. Sara's bedroom was upstairs while Dagger's living quarters were downstairs. Simon constantly reminded him of the number of stairs from the first floor to Sara's bedroom.

Sara tossed that letter aside and picked up another. "Hmmmm, here's a woman who claims her husband was kidnapped by aliens and replaced by one of their own."

"We'll get Skizzy on that one. He'll believe whatever the woman says." His eyes swept to where Sara was leaning on the wooden ledge surrounding his work area. Waist length hair in a myriad of colors ranging from black to auburn to blonde drifted down her arms. Plum-colored slacks hugged every curve of her body. He dragged his thoughts to the empty suitcase in his bedroom. It had been his plan since their last case that once he was back on his feet he would leave. The more he stuck around, the more in danger everyone would be. Every time he even entertained the thought of packing his suitcase, Sara always gave him a subtle reminder how he was no longer in danger from BettaTec. She never tried to talk him out of packing. Matter of fact, on more than one occasion she had offered to help. Maybe once his razor burn healed he would pack.

"Here's one." Sara straightened and turned from the desk. "A fourteen-month cold case. Kara Jensen claims her husband, Rick, left for a business meeting in Miami but never made it."

"Him and two thousand other bored husbands."

"Not really. His car was found on Fenton Road with a flat tire."

"I'm sure Padre and his team of crack detectives investigated that one thoroughly. If Padre didn't find anything, no one will."

"Well, they didn't find anything and the wife is desperate." Sara shoved the sleeves up on her pink sweater as she carried the letter to the couch. He noticed how the clothes she wore blended with the decor. Mauve and pink flowers could be found in the fabric of just about every piece of furniture and the area rug. It made his eyeballs ache. Dagger's idea of color was a lighter shade of gray. Black and gray were about all he ever dressed in.

"Look." Sara held up a picture of a blue-eyed baby with a pink floral band in her hair. "She was only six-months old when he left. The wife claims Rick would walk over hot coals for Bella. Whenever he traveled he always contacted her on the web cam to say goodnight."

"Yeah, cute kid. I still say hubby found a warm body

to cling to. It wouldn't be the first time a husband suddenly is a father and not quite liking the role. You do remember Scott Peterson, right?"

"Except he didn't disappear. His pregnant wife did."

"Yeah, but some men feel impending fatherhood puts a crimp in their freedom. Jensen made it look like he met with some ill-fate, but probably abandoned his car and hopped on a motorcycle he stashed nearby and took off. Were his bank accounts cleaned out?"

Sara skimmed the rest of the letter. "Don't know. We'd have to ask Padre. Poor woman. Without a body she can't even claim the insurance money to live on."

"Ah, money. The root of all evil." He swung his legs off the table and sat up.

"Speaking of money, we haven't made any in the last two months." Sara sat down on the coffee table facing him. "You know, the green stuff."

Money was the last of their worries. Dagger had tons of it from previous jobs, both legal and questionable. He paid Sara rent for his share of the house and a salary as his assistant at Dagger Investigations. But money had never been high on Sara's list of wants. If anything, he had created a Robin to his Batman, a Tonto to his Cochise. She had instincts better than his and talents he could never do without. Sara's only problem was boredom. He studied those turquoise eyes, flawless skin, and sultry lips and had to keep reminding himself not to mix business with pleasure. It didn't help that every other word out of Simon's mouth told him to go for it before someone else nabbed her.

Dagger pulled the letter from Sara's grasp and heaved out a lengthy sigh. "I was really getting used to lounging around."

"I noticed."

He skimmed the letter and studied the picture of Kara and Bella Jensen. "Okay. Have Skizzy hack into the police department records and print out everything they've got. Then we can discuss the case over lunch."

8 The man lay face down in a shallow ditch seventy yards from the mansion. It was obvious from the path of bent and twisted foliage that he had barreled through a thick patch of underbrush. Around his neck was a silk scarf with bold red flowers against a black background. His hands had been duct-taped behind his back. Leyton was the last to arrive, fearful of what he might find.

"It's a man, sir," Sergeant Jackson assured him. The patrolmen parted as Leyton pulled to a stop next to Padre and Wozniak.

Padre studied the ground between the ditch and the mansion. It looked as though a herd of elephants had trampled the area; and with all the rain last night, any indication of what direction the deceased might have come from had been washed away. The sky overhead didn't look promising. Clouds were a low ceiling of threatening gray, hardly moving as though too heavy to keep aloft and looking for a place to rest.

Wozniak turned to a young officer who looked ready to blow lunch. "Contact headquarters. Have them send Luther out here. Then call the building department. I want blueprints of the Sebold mansion and property."

The officer stole a quick glance back at the deceased

with its bluish tinge and distorted grimace. He swallowed quick and with a nod hurried off to the squad car to call it in.

"Let's fan out, people," Wozniak yelled. "This is now a crime scene."

A loud scream ripped through the air. Venus flattened both hands against her mouth as though jamming the scream back down her throat.

"All of you." Wozniak motioned to the IPI members. "Do you recognize this man?"

Flea's eyes had doubled in size. If he couldn't handle a dead body, how could he handle a ghost? "Never saw him before."

"Lurch? What about you?"

"Huh?" Josh suddenly realized the chief was referring to him. "Uh, no. Other than the three of us and the reporter, we haven't seen anyone else around." He took a step closer and chuckled. "Didn't the Boston Strangler tie bows?"

Venus recovered enough to take a second look at the deceased. "Oh my gods and goddesses. The scarf." She forced herself to study the fabric wrapped around the dead man's neck. "It's hers. I complimented Sheila on the scarf. It matched her black leather pants and red cashmere sweater. She was wearing it last night."

9 With the ghost hunters sequestered back on the couch under the watchful eye of Sergeant Jackson, the eight officers combing the surrounding area, and Cedar Point's medical examiner, Luther Jamison, outside with the body, Padre and John secluded themselves in the dining room off the kitchen, pages of blueprints unrolled on the polished mahogany table. The room could easily accommodate a dinner for twenty. Ornate pictures of shipping vessels and the harbor decorated the walls. The room needed two chandeliers of tear drop lights to illuminate the length of the table.

"Who gave the ghost hunters permission to investigate this house?" John set a brass bookend of a horse's head at each corner of the paper to keep it from rolling back up.

"An attorney for the estate. Some guy by the name of Jason Godfrey. He's in California. Contracted a company over the years to keep the grounds looking halfway decent. However, once the Historical Society moved out and the economy took a dive, he let everything go." Padre ran a finger through the dust on the table. A web hung from one chandelier to the other and Padre kept waiting for it to drift down over their heads. "It's obvious he didn't spend money to keep the interior clean."

John focused on the film of dust collecting in the

corners of the room. "The upkeep for a mansion this size costs an arm and a leg. Any idea what we're looking at?" John asked.

"I have Peters and Cromwell working on finding out which real estate office had the account the last time the place rented out."

A voice boomed from the doorway. "Why the hell isn't this house being searched more thoroughly?" Leyton demanded. "My daughter could be unconscious and stuffed in a closet somewhere."

John straightened and tried to keep his voice under control. "My men already searched all of the rooms, Leyton. All they could find was her jacket and purse, nothing stolen. They didn't find any blood in any of the rooms. I need them outside for now until we have studied the blueprints. I would suggest you stay in the foyer or in the library where the rest of the people are. Padre and I will do another search for any panic rooms or vaults added after the house was built, but we need to study the blue prints first."

"I can't just sit by doing nothing. You have to let me help."

"I'm a father. I understand your need to do something, but you have to face the fact, Leyton, that any clues you might find would be questionable. I'm sorry to say this, but as long as it's your daughter's scarf around the dead man's neck, your daughter is not only a missing person, but she is a suspect."

"WHAT?! You can't possibly be serious." He charged into the dining room like a rhino, but John held up one hand.

"It would behoove you to stay outside on the veranda. If you can't stay out of the way, then I will have to have an officer escort you back to Cedar Point. I don't care how many threats you make to contact the mayor, your lawyer, or a local member of Congress. We are wasting valuable time keeping you under control and out of the way."

Leyton looked to Padre as if the lowly sergeant would have any say in the matter. All Padre did was shrug. "It's for the best. You're a newspaperman. Put yourself in our shoes. How would you write the story if Sheila wasn't involved? You would be all over the cops for not controlling the investigation. Perhaps it's best if you go back to your house or keep busy at the office. We'll let you know if anything develops. Sooner or later other newspapers are going to hear about this and they are going to have a lot of questions for you. Right now this entire area is blocked off and, knock on wood, we haven't seen any press people. But we can't keep a lid on this forever."

Leyton looked dejected. His shoulders hunched and his bottom lip started to quiver. It was possible the burly guy was going to breakdown and cry. "She's my only child," he whispered.

John and Padre locked eyes across the table in silent frustration. They were wasting a lot of time here. John grabbed the walkie-talkie and clicked it on. "Porter."

"Sir?"

"Check for any underground shelters or root cellars. And have Luther update me as soon as he is finished out there."

John set the walkie-talkie down and looked at Leyton. "You know anything about reading blueprints?"

Leyton blinked quickly, realizing he wasn't being exiled from the premises. "Uh, yes. I worked in the building department during my high school days. I think I remember a thing or two." He pulled out a chair and bent his hulking frame over the table. "This the first floor?"

"Yes. So far my men haven't found any escape tunnels, but that doesn't mean some renovations haven't been done on the inside. Examine the blue print and see if you can spot any anomalies." John picked up the walkie-talkie again. "Sergeant Jackson?"

"Jackson here."

"Would you have each of our guests write up a detailed report of everything that transpired last night. We won't interview them again until we get them back to the precinct." Voices could be heard in the background.

"Why do we have to stick around?"

"Why can't we go home?"

"You can't hold us against our will."

"We didn't do anything."

"This house has bad karma."

John clicked the walkie-talkie again. "The faster they start writing, the sooner they can get to the precinct and receive a meal. They are the last people to see Miss Monroe. Their lack of cooperation would not look good for any future business they hope to attract." John set the walkie-talkie down.

Luther came to an abrupt stop in the doorway. He took a moment to take in the banquet size room. His gaze was slow, almost analytical. He may as well have been looking for the heart, lung, and kidneys of the mansion. "Holy shit. By the size and age of this house I expected a *hired help enter here* sign on a back door. Probably the first time a black man entered through the front door." His thin frame held up a head of enormous brain cells.

"Let's hear it," John said.

He advanced and stopped in front of the table. "No wallet or any other identification on the man. I'd say he's in his thirties, been dead less than twelve hours. That scarf was tied on pretty tight but I found bruising on the neck, blood under the deceased's fingernails. He put up a fight. There's a bump on the side of his head. He might have been knocked out first. The scarf was wrapped around his neck twice, tied in a knot, then in a bow. Really weird. Like a Christmas package. An image of what looked like the Liberty Bell was tattooed on his upper right arm. Looks fresh. Other than that, won't know more til we get him back on the steel."

A young man dressed in all white entered the room and set a large thermos, a stack of drinking cups and a box of donuts on the table. "Did you want them here, Doc?"

"Yes. Thanks, Phil." He turned to John. "Thought you guys could use some coffee so I had Phil make a mercy run."

"You are a god, Luther," John said.

"Any suspects?" Luther poured cups of coffee and passed them around.

"Got three ghost hunters by the staircase." Padre blew on the steaming cup of coffee, then took a tentative sip.

"Ghost hunters?" Luther's wide smile revealed a mouth of perfect white teeth. "With the storm from hell that blew in last night they were searching for ghosts?"

"Yeah, and Sheila Monroe was with them. She's still missing." Padre pawed through the box of donuts until he found a chocolate one.

Luther looked at Leyton Monroe and shook his head. "Sorry. Wish I could have better news for you. Forensics couldn't find much with the water-soaked ground. Any footprints are washed away. Can't even tell what direction the man came from or if he was dumped."

"Well, he certainly couldn't have walked from the house and my daughter couldn't possibly have carried him."

"Actually, he could have stumbled from the house or even the street. The way he was laying face down in the ditch makes it appear that he was stumbling or walking and didn't see the ditch. He couldn't have walked far in his condition."

"What about satellite surveillance?" Leyton said with renewed enthusiasm. "The victim pulls up to the house, someone kills him, Sheila witnesses it, and the killer takes her and the car and they drive off. They'd have it on satellite, right? The killer is probably miles away by now, maybe left Sheila unconscious somewhere else."

Padre looked at John and they both knew it was a long shot with the storm last night, but to placate Leyton, John said, "I'll call it in, see if anything was picked up on satellite. It would explain why we can't find Sheila. Maybe she stepped out for a cigarette and the deceased and the killer were driving together and stopped for directions, or pulled off in the storm."

10 Sara munched on a piece of fruit in silence as she read through the missing persons report on Rick Jensen. Dagger watched the intensity in her eyes. The remains of his greasy hamburger were on his plate. He sat with his hands hidden under the table, playing with his pocket knife. He drew the blade slowly across the top of his hand and watched as blood seeped quickly from the cut. He wiped the blood with a napkin and smiled as the cut quickly closed, leaving barely a hint that he had injured himself. A second cut, this time slower and deeper. When he turned his arm and pressed the knife to his wrist, Sara had had enough.

"That vein will spray blood all over the floor before the injury heals. And if you get blood on my new leather jacket, you're buying me a new one."

Dagger flicked his gaze to Sara. Her leather jacket hung on the back of her chair. It was a sunflower or buttercup yellow. He never could get his shades right. And blood red would definitely stain the leather. He snapped the knife closed and put it back in his pocket.

"You are having way too much fun with that," Sara pointed out. It was after his injury in Nebraska when a doctor used several pints of Sara's blood to save Dagger's life that they realized he now had almost the same healing abilities that Sara possessed. He, of course, couldn't regenerate limbs the way Sara could. Nor could he shapeshift. But the ability to heal was the only thing that saved his life in Nebraska.

"What can I say? It's better than one of those Wii games." They sat near the fireplace at Northwoods, a huge log cabin restaurant near the outskirts of Cedar Point. He lost count of the number of men whose eyes had drifted to his partner, how even the gray skies couldn't dull the brightness of her eyes. She didn't need tons of makeup to enhance her natural beauty. But there was only so much a man could take. All he had to do was level dark eyes on the drooling admirers to send them scurrying in the other direction. It was more his dark mood and the bulge of the Kimber .45 under the leather jacket than his sinister glare that kept them at a distance.

"Quit with the death rays already," Sara said without looking up from the report.

Damn. Nothing got by his partner. He should know by now she didn't need protection. Simon said Dagger had a streak of jealousy in his veins since the first day Sara caught the eye of the rich homegrown playboy, Nick Tyler. But Nick made the mistake of assuming Sara's interest in him was love and he had tried to pull a stealth engagement on her, choosing a venue of two hundred close friends and the press to pop the question. Once Sara caught wind of his intentions, she was furious. First, his plan was hatched by Sheila Monroe, Dagger's ex-fiancee. And second, he wanted to be engaged for four or five years which would keep Sara out of circulation while Nick continued his playboy reputation. But there had been a third reason Nick's plan failed. Sara didn't love him.

"Listen to this," Sara said. "Rick Jensen's appointment in Miami claimed he never showed up yet his ticket was used at O'Hare Airport."

"What did I tell you? He ran."

"Without any money? It says in the report that the Jensen savings accounts and 401Ks were never touched."

"He had been squirreling away money, a safety stash. Every guy, and sometimes even girl, does it."

Sara gazed over the sheets of paper. "Like all those gym bags of cash you have hidden in the spare tire compartment of each of your cars?"

He looked quickly to see if anyone was seated too close to their table, then leaned across and whispered, "Which is a quarter of a million short since you gave the one bag to that doctor out in Nebraska."

"A doctor who saved your life," she snapped. Sara returned her attention to the report. "After checking airport security cameras it was determined that the person using Rick Jensen's ticket wasn't Rick Jensen. Mark Ettle was on summer break from Purdue Calumet College and claims he found the airline ticket on the side of the road when he stopped to check the air in his bicycle's tire."

"Probably a lie."

"It was. After intense interrogation..."

"Damn," Dagger interrupted. "The cops used the tire iron again."

"After intense interrogation Mark admitted he took it from Jensen's car which was parked on the side of the road."

"Strange. Why didn't he steal the car?"

"He said he wasn't a thief, and besides..."

"He didn't know how to hot wire a car." Dagger flashed a smile behind his French fry. "Did everything else check out with Mark the thief?"

"Yes. He arrived in Miami with very little money, hooked up with some girls who had a room at one of the resort hotels. They confirmed that he was traveling on a shoestring budget."

"So he didn't take Jensen's wallet."

"Right. If he had seen Jensen or was the one who had killed him and buried his body, he would have had all of Jensen's money. Kara says Rick had three credit cards and five hundred dollars."

"Did anyone use Jensen's credit cards after he went missing?"

"No."

But that wasn't surprising. Just by watching television even the dumbest of thieves knew that the first thing cops did was check for any activity on a credit card, and with cameras at ATM machines they can get a clear picture of the thief.

"What do you think? Should we call and meet with Kara?"

Dagger pushed his plate away which was quickly snatched by a waitress who was already balancing several empty plates in one arm. "Can I get you anything else?" she asked.

"Coffee and one hot tea when you have a chance."

When the waitress left he returned his attention to Sara's question. "Not yet. Skizzy is still working on the rest of the reports and I want to ask Padre a few questions first, find out if anyone is still actively working the case. Who was the detective?"

Sara flipped through to the end of the report. "Miles Vector. Ever hear of him?"

"No."

Sara pushed her plate away just as the waitress deposited their hot drinks. "I hate days like this. I can't keep the chill off." Sara turned toward the fireplace and rubbed her hands.

"We've had enough rain to convince Skizzy to start building an ark. It's the dampness that seeps through the bones, intensifies every ache and pain." Dagger instinctively touched the back of his neck where he could feel the scar. "We should try Padre first." He pulled out his phone and handed it to Sara. "Send him a text message to call me when he has a chance. Those damn buttons are too small for my fingers. I swear they make these toys for fingers no bigger than a kid's."

One perfect eyebrow shot up as Sara started punching in the message with her two thumbs. "Maybe you old folks should stick to smoke signals." Her fingers were long, the nails shaped but polish free. Sara wasn't one for fake glamour under pounds of makeup. She was as natural and genuine in image as well as in spirit. "All done," she announced and handed Dagger's cell phone back to him.

"Let me see that report." Dagger skimmed through it, his eyes picking out only the significant words. "He worked for a trade exhibit company. No big company secrets there to put him in danger. No work-related problems. Neighbors say they were a loving couple. Yeah, right."

"So sinister."

"There's no such thing as a perfect couple. A wife secretly makes R-rated tapes for the Internet. A husband likes to beat his wife or crawl in bed with his daughter. That's why I don't take cases dealing with domestic problems. Too many lies, too many secrets. Doesn't matter if they are rich or poor. If you look close enough, everyone has flaws." He waved the report at her. "And if we dig deep enough, we are going to find that the Jensens have something to hide."

"So you don't want to help her out."

"I just think we need to find out more from the reporting officer before we start spinning our wheels."

11 "Where did you park them?" Chief Wozniak sank onto his leather chair and washed a hand over his face.

"They each have their own little room and a cup of coffee, although Venus claims the furniture is positioned wrong because her feng shui is all out of whack." Padre tossed his notepad on the desk and threw himself into a chair. "Damn I'm tired."

"Feng shui, huh? Why us?"

"God is punishing us for leaving the seminary. That's what it is, John."

"Well, he is certainly making our lives challenging."

They had left the forensics crew to do a more thorough scouring of the mansion only to placate Leyton. The blueprints and wall pounding hadn't revealed any hidden rooms, tunnels, or walkways. A flashlight had been found under a cabinet in the foyer. Josh had identified it as one of the ones he had brought. If Sheila was anywhere in the mansion, conscious or unconscious, they hadn't been able to find her. Leyton Monroe had returned to his office, although he wasn't happy about it. He wanted to do a television appeal and offer a reward for information leading to the whereabouts of his daughter. Chief Wozniak talked him out of the reward for now. They would have every lunatic in the country calling with false information and the cops would be chasing after erroneous leads.

"What about the lie detectors? Did the ghost hunters agree to it?" Padre asked.

"At first, no. Josh started spouting off civil rights violations, but I convinced him in my most gracious voice that it wouldn't look good for his business if the newspapers reported that his members were uncooperative in a murder investigation."

"Who's doing it, Keene?"

"Yeah. We're bringing in food for all three and Keene will take them one at a time. Then I'll have them interviewed separately, get their formal statements again. We need to keep them here as long as possible. Something happened in that house. If we turn them loose too soon, Leyton will be on the phone with Chief Loughton, the Board of Police and Fire Commissioners, our state senators, and any other contact he has."

"You don't want me to interview any of them?"

"I think they are getting pretty sick of both of us. I want you to get a front row seat at the autopsy. Get those prints processed. See if we can find a name for the deceased." The chief's intercom buzzed. "Wozniak... put him through." John nodded at Padre. "It's the estate attorney, Jason Godfrey." John punched the speaker phone and introduced himself and Padre. He told Godfrey briefly about the case. "Is there anything you can tell me about the estate? Were any renovations done that are not on the current blueprints?"

Godfrey spoke in a slow relaxed tempo. They could

hear water splashing in the background and wondered if Godfrey was floating in a pool somewhere. "Not that I was made aware of. The place has been a money drain." They could hear him sipping something and then inhaling, probably sucking on a cigar. "Hasn't been occupied since the Historical Society rented out the place a number of years ago." Another sip and a large splash with giggling could be heard in the background. One could only imagine a warm California sun and fancy umbrella drinks pool side.

"Did anyone have a key to the place?" Padre asked.

"Amy Parker of Colonial Realty has the only key. She was the one who contacted me about the ghost hunters. I thought it would be good publicity, maybe get that white elephant off my books." In the background they could hear Godfrey ask someone to get him another mimosa. John checked his watch and lifted his eyebrows. Godfrey was drinking rather early but it was California.

"How much is the house worth?" John asked.

"Usually whatever someone is willing to pay. But it is valued at twenty-five million. It is a fabulous piece of history. When it was on the market I had a service in there keeping the place spit shined. But it costs too much to keep that place maintained. The fireplaces haven't been used in decades because of the cost of insurance."

Padre said, "The house must have some history if the ghost hunters were investigating it. Do you know of any occurrences?"

Godfrey barked out a laugh. "Thanks, babe," he whispered to someone. "Any house with gargoyles and turrets or older than fifty years is going to have rumors of strange happenings, but no, not since I have been handling the estate. Plus, I don't listen to rumors. I deal in cold hard cash."

"But it certainly could get this white elephant off your hands if something sensational happened," John started, "say like a wealthy heiress disappearing."

There was silence for a few beats. "What are you suggesting, Chief? Do you think I paid this IPI group to kidnap someone for headlines?"

"I have to look at all possibilities and right now we are running out of time. If there is some panic room or vault not on the blue prints, we need to know now." John stared at Padre across the desk as the silence stretched.

"Tell you what," Godfrey finally said, "how about we ignore this whole line of questioning and I don't sue your ass, the department, and the city." With that Godfrey hung up.

"Guess that was a no," Padre said.

"Hell, I hate the guy for the sun, the pool, and the naked ladies paddling around while we're here swimming in dead end clues, a missing person, and a dead body."

Padre checked his phone before heading out. He had three messages. One was a text message from Dagger to call him. If Luther wasn't ready for him, Padre would take some time to return calls.

12 Sheila moved slowly through the dining room, going from chair to chair, fearful of walking without the benefit of something to hold onto. She had checked the kitchen for an aspirin or even an ice pack but the cabinets were empty and a refrigerator was non-existent. Maybe if she just laid down for a few minutes her headache would start to subside. Whether the mud had hardened outside or not, the minute she could walk without the world spinning, she was going to walk to the nearest gas station.

She made her way down the hall and back to the study. Sheila closed the shutters on the windows but it only helped to block out a third of the light. She stretched out on the couch and closed her eyes. But sleep wouldn't come. She sensed movement in the air but was afraid to open her eyes. Was that the sound of someone breathing that she heard? Slowly Sheila opened her eyes to find a girl standing next to the couch. She bolted to a sitting position, then grabbed her sore head and winced.

"Sorry. I didn't mean to wake you."

The girl had corn silk hair that hung down her back. Blue eyes were framed by long lashes. She was dressed in an old-fashioned pinafore-type dress and patent leather shoes. Sheila firmly believed she had finally met Alice and she was definitely in Wonderland.

"Who are you?"

"Colleen."

Where had the girl been hiding while Sheila was knocked out cold on the couch? And how did Sheila get to the couch? There wasn't any possible way this girl could have carried her.

"How old are you?" She moved aside and motioned toward the couch. Colleen was careful not to wrinkle her dress when she sat. It reminded Sheila of when her mother had sent her to a finishing school with other six-year-olds so they could learn which fork to use and how to act like a young lady in public. Sheila had even had a pair of white socks bordered with lace like Colleen wore.

"Seven," Colleen replied. "How old are you?"

Sheila smiled. "Older than seven. Much older."

"You're pretty."

"Thank you. So are you." Sheila wasn't sure how much information she could get out of a seven-year-old, but girls, as she well knew, could sometimes be very chatty. "How long have I been here?"

Colleen didn't reply, just raised her shoulders in an *I don't know* gesture.

So if the girl didn't know, who would? "Do you know how I got here?"

The girl leaned close and whispered, "It was the storm."

The storm? What did that mean? Last night's storm? "I don't understand." *Why would that have anything to do with why I'm no longer at the Sebold mansion?* she thought. Somewhere in the house a door slammed. Heavy footsteps could be heard coming from upstairs.

Colleen's eyes widened. "Hide. He's coming."

"Who?" Sheila rose slowly and turned toward the hallway, the footsteps growing closer. "Who is coming?" But when she returned her gaze to the couch, Colleen was gone.

Sheila considered running to the dining room to see if there were any knives in the buffet. Whoever was coming down the hall might have been the one who hit her over the head and drove her to whatever town they were in. She wasn't even sure they were in the same state any more. But it was too late.

A figure stopped in the doorway and smiled. "Glad to see you have awakened."

Sheila was speechless. She had to be dreaming or she stumbled into a Shakespearean play. She might have been attracted to the man in a turn of the century sort of way. His hair was long and touched the collar of his white shirt. His suit coat had tails, like something a groom would wear to a wedding. The face was attractive enough, but the eyes exuded a danger bordering on curiosity and threat.

She straightened her back and glared at him. "Who are you and how did I get here? I demand you take me home immediately."

The man smiled slowly then threw back his head and laughed. "Wouldn't that we all would like to go home." He bowed his head slightly and said, "I am Adrian Walker, madam. And who might you be?"

"Sheila Monroe. I am a reporter with the *Daily*

Herald."

"Ahhh. A newspaper. I have always wanted to tell someone my life story." He motioned to the couch. "Sit. Please."

Sheila remained standing. "I want answers. Where am I and how did I get here?"

"And you will get your answers, in good stead."

Who talks this way anymore? Sheila wondered. *As a matter of fact, who even dresses like that anymore?*

"Let's start with how I got here." Sheila slowly sat down, afraid any fast motions would set the room spinning again. She moved back against the cushions and folded her arms across her chest.

"You literally fell into my lap." He lowered himself onto the couch and crossed his legs, taking time to straighten the crease in his slacks. He moved with the elegance of an aristocrat and even spoke with an accent she couldn't quite detect. "Bumped your head when you fell."

Sheila touched her forehead and then the back of her head which were still tender to the touch. "I could have a concussion. I should have gone to the hospital and had X-rays. Besides, I may have fallen, but I certainly didn't walk to whatever town I'm in. I will ask again. Where am I?"

"Dawson's Corner," he replied simply as though he should have added, "where else?"

"Is that in Indiana?"

"Of course. Now my turn."

"I wasn't aware we were playing a game."

When he smiled his eyes appeared even darker and

more mysterious. "I love games. It sometimes gets very boring in this," his eyes took on an edge of delight, "town." He pulled an object from his pocket and held it up. "Please tell me what this gadget is."

Sheila took it from him and almost squealed with relief. "It's a cell phone." But it wasn't hers. She pushed the power button but the screen said service was unavailable.

"A phone you carry in your pocket? Interesting."

"What's interesting is that you sound as though you have never seen a cell phone before."

"There are a lot of things we've missed out on living in isolation the way we do. How does it work?"

"Mainly you need a cell phone tower nearby to get reception, but don't ask me for specifics. All I know is I push a button and I can talk to anyone anywhere in the world."

Adrian took the phone back and studied it. "Anywhere in the world? How utterly delightful."

"My phone even has Internet connection so I can check Emails, download music, books, photos."

"Music? Books?" He studied the size of the phone, turning it over in his hand. "How does one get a book out of a tiny thing like this?"

Now Sheila knew where she had heard his accent. It was somewhat British with a little gothic vampire tossed in for good measure, sprinkled with some *Pride and Prejudice*. Was Sheila dreaming? She pinched a fold of skin between her thumb and index finger and winced as her nails dug in. "You don't know what the Internet is, do you?"

His gaze shifted from her to the phone and back to her. "Afraid I'm not too familiar with a lot of new technology."

Sheila looked around the room at the expensive paintings and furniture. "Yet you don't appear to be without."

Adrian followed her gaze and dipped his head in agreement. "Most of it wasn't mine. Guess you can say I borrowed them piece by piece."

Sheila straightened her back and gave a haughty look down her nose, something she had learned from her father. "If it's a ransom you want, my father is rich and will pay any amount of money."

Adrian threw back his head again and laughed, thoroughly enjoying himself. "Money is of no use to me."

Sheila felt deflated and for a second wondered where the child's mother was and if Adrian had set up some type of commune with scores of women upstairs popping out babies every year. For some reason the phrase, "come into my parlor said the spider to the fly" ran through her head.

"Then what is it you want?" Sheila demanded as she scrambled her addled brain to remember her self defense classes.

He turned the cell phone over in his hand and then settled his gaze on Sheila. "I want to learn about these and any other technology I have missed out on."

13

"Okay, let's have it." Padre sidled over to the examining table. Luther had just finished suturing the body of John Doe.

"The victim is in his early thirties, sixty-nine inches tall, and one hundred and seventy pounds. He was in relatively good health, had recently consumed approximately three cups of coffee, scrambled eggs and a cinnamon roll, but whether he had any drugs or alcohol in his system we won't know until we get the tox screen back. Should have some good fingerprints to process. He was strangled with the scarf but it was a slow death. If his hands hadn't been bound he would have been able to get the scarf off, in my opinion. At least, if it were me I would have attempted to tear the thing off."

"So death is ruled a homicide," Padre wrote, "as though there were any doubt." He bent down for a closer look at the tattoo. "Any other scars or markings?"

"As I mentioned previously, the tattoo was no more than two days old. There was a vaccination on the upper left arm. He might have been overseas at some point in his life. With any luck, he might be ex-military so we might be able to I.D. him pretty quickly."

"No gang markings?"

"No prison tats either. Hands aren't calloused so he

probably worked a desk job. How many names are on your missing persons' log?"

"In Cedar Point, about twenty-four over the past year but this guy could be from anywhere. I'll start with home grown missing persons and then expand it to the surrounding states. Find anything else on him?"

"If you were looking for money or a passport stuffed in a sock you are out of luck."

Padre walked over to a side table where John Doe's clothes were laid out. There was a blue checkered shirt, crisp new denim jeans marred with mud and grass stains, and a simple gold wedding band. "No engraving on the ring. That narrows the search to those that were married."

Luther looked up from the examining table. "Some divorced people refuse to take off their rings. Same for widows and widowers."

"Good point."

"What did your people find out by the mansion?"

"Not a thing. No clue as to whether or not the deceased was in the mansion. No abandoned cars anywhere in the area. No sign of Sheila Monroe anywhere either. I don't suppose you got fingerprints off of that scarf."

"Yeah, right. We'll get those TV *CSI* folks on that right away." Luther stripped out of his apron and gloves and motioned Padre out of the room. "Let's assume Miss Monroe wasn't involved in the murder, even though the scarf was tied in a very feminine bow. Does the M.O. sound like anything you had heard of before?"

"Other than the suggestion it was the Boston Strangler?" Padre said with a laugh. "I've got my guys checking into it."

"What about those ghost hunters? Any of them have skeletons in their closets?" Luther flashed a smile. "No pun intended."

"So far, no, but we aren't done turning them inside out yet."

Luther scribbled his name on the bottom of a report, ran the pages through a copier, and handed one copy to Padre. "Keep me posted."

14 Dagger turned the key fob over in his hand then played with the switch. "Not bad. And how do I keep from accidentally flicking the damn thing on and shooting my nuts off?"

Skizzy narrowed his eyes at him and drawled, "Now that would be pretty hard seeing that you'd need a large enough target."

Sara stifled a smile as their squirrely friend remained stoic.

"It does have a safety if you'd spend more time inspecting my hard work."

Dagger glared at Skizzy over the top of the key fob. "And here we didn't think you had a sense of humor." He pocketed the fob and motioned with his fingers in a gimme gesture. "What did you find out?"

"Yeah, yeah. Hold your britches." Strands of graying hair were wrestling their way free from Skizzy's ponytail. Skizzy's mode of dress consisted of a tee shirt and camouflage pants. No one knew for sure if Skizzy still had fifty-two cards in his mental deck, whether his head was still scrambled from Viet Nam or being a recluse made him suspicious of everything and everyone except for a select few. Skizzy was a paranoid schizophrenic and believed Big Brother was keeping tabs on him, that the powers that be have inserted tracking chips in every baby born and anyone who had ever been in the hospital in the past five years. And when it was recently discovered that Dagger had a chip in his neck, that confirmed all of Skizzy's suspicions.

Sara roamed the pawn shop, wondering why people would part with heirlooms, gold watches, pocket knives, and other gems that were nothing more than garage sale items. She poked at what looked like a turtle shell, expecting something to pop out from underneath.

Skizzy emerged from the back room and set several sheets of paper on the counter.

"What is this, Skizzy?" Sara asked. "It looks like a turtle shell."

Skizzy gave a quick glance at where she was pointing. "It's a turtle shell."

"Why on earth would you give anyone money for a turtle shell?"

"Knowing Skizzy," Dagger said, "it's probably a listening device or a weapon of some sort."

Sara moved away from the shell and joined Dagger at the counter where he was skimming Skizzy's report. "That's all?" Sara asked.

"The dick who worked the case is now retired and I didn't find any forwarding address for him. At least he isn't living in Cedar Point," Skizzy reported.

"But I bet you traced his Social Security number." Dagger scanned the pages.

Skizzy eyed him with a smile. His eyes wobbled as though barely tethered to his body and they rarely looked in the same direction. "I was able to find out where his Social Security checks are mailed." He handed Dagger a slip of paper with a postal box address in Arkansas.

"That doesn't sound promising. With a postal box, that tells me he travels a lot and his mail gets forwarded. I don't suppose…"

Skizzy's eyebrows danced. "Found his son in Austin, Texas. Your retired cop probably spends the winters in Texas." He handed another piece of paper to Dagger. "I'm surprised you aren't out looking for your missing ex-fiancee."

"Sheila?" Dagger was surprised he hadn't heard anything in the news seeing how connected Sheila's father was.

"Heard it on the police scanner. Don't know why you don't keep yours on."

"He hasn't turned it on since we returned from Nebraska," Sara confessed. "You would think our house was a monastery with the silence he has insisted."

"You make it sound like I commanded it." But Dagger wasn't thinking about his mood or the police scanner. He was thinking about how Sara just referred to her house as *our* house. "So what's this about Sheila?"

"All I learned from the police scanner is that she was last seen at some mansion outside of town with a group of ghost hunters. They didn't find her but they found another body on the property. Obviously the rich have pull because not only were our boys in blue dispatched to the scene, but *Daddy Warbucks* has also demanded the National Guard and search dogs."

15

Padre was eating a fast food hamburger at nine o'clock at night as he watched the forensics crew examine Sheila's Jaguar in the precinct garage. Detective Joe Spagnola strolled over, hands in his pockets, and stopped at the railing next to Padre.

"Anything?" Joe asked. His suit would have cost Padre one week's pay. And his shirt had Joe's initials monogrammed on the cuff. Although Joe always had excellent taste in clothes, Padre was sure Sheila had picked out the shirt and tie. Rumors had been floating for years that Joe was on the take, but they were always lacking proof. Padre knew Joe didn't gamble, had little regard for lawbreakers so it was doubtful Joe would do anything illegal. Joe wasn't unlike a lot of cops who became detectives and vied to dress the part. Joe was single, didn't have normal expenses like Padre who had a wife who was always redecorating and boys who were active in school sports. It was no wonder the cuffs on Padre's shirts and pants were frayed. He was a poor man's *Columbo*.

"Not a clue. It's a real puzzle. Leyton is trying to hire an entire kennel of cadaver-sniffing dogs for tomorrow. The mayor is half up the police chief's ass who has his shoe up Chief Wozniak's ass who has his boot on my neck."

"Who can blame him? Sheila's his only child."

"An only child who is a spoiled brat. When she was twelve she ran away from home because her father wouldn't buy her a pony. What did he refuse to buy her this time?"

"Believe me, Sheila wouldn't have left her silver Jaguar sitting there."

"Why not? She trades them in as often as I change my underwear." Padre tossed the empty wrapper and bag in the garbage.

Joe took out a pack of gum and held it out to Padre.

"Thanks." He took a stick and unwrapped it, one of his numerous attempts to quit smoking.

Joe unwrapped a stick and shoved it in his mouth. Padre studied the detective trying to assess the true relationship between him and Sheila. A cop wasn't the kind of guy Padre could picture with the rich heiress. Joe was old world Italian and looked more like a member of the Sopranos. Sheila picked boyfriends that went against everything her father pictured in a future son-in-law. The worst had been Chase Dagger. Leyton Monroe had tried to dig up everything he could on Dagger, but all the earth-moving equipment in the world couldn't excavate his background. Padre could only assume the more Dagger kept Sheila at arm's length, the more she wanted him. But Dagger was distant and cold and had very few close friends. The more dangerous and mysterious the man, the more Sheila was intrigued.

"How were things between the two of you, Joe?"

Joe chewed the gum slowly as the forensics crew slammed the trunk lid shut on the Jaguar. Padre had already questioned Joe earlier and was satisfied the detective couldn't add anything to the mystery of Sheila's disappearance.

"I don't hit women, if that's what you're asking."

"That wasn't what I was asking."

"Her old man already grilled me, or tried to. Sheila is an enigma. She's independent yet needy. She's a daddy's girl, but fights him every step of the way. She manipulates men, or tries to. We aren't exclusive, but I'm not dating anyone else. Can't say the same about her. I don't see her everyday. We don't talk everyday, so as far as I know she could be seeing other people.

"Do you love her?"

He seemed to taste those words in his mouth, choosing his response carefully. "I don't kid myself that she could ever have a future with someone who wasn't of her social status. If she broke up with me tomorrow, I'd be fine with that. Whatever she wants." He waited several beats, chewing his gum and snapping it like a truck stop waitress, a habit that had always annoyed Sheila. Then his face turned serious as he added, "Yeah, I love her."

Searchlights lit up the front of the Sebold mansion. One cop leaned against a squad car smoking a cigarette. Crime scene tape fluttered around a section of the north property where the body had been found. Police units had been unsuccessful in finding any sign of Sheila Monroe and had suspended further searching until tomorrow.

The rain had ended a couple hours ago but more storms were due to blow in tomorrow. High above the house the gray hawk drew a tight circle searching for movement or just for humans, alive or dead.

How's it going?

Sara heard Dagger's words in her head. *Just one cop guarding the property. There aren't any lights on in the house. I can see crime scene tape surrounding a ditch. Skizzy didn't say if the police identified the victim, did he?*

No. Just that it wasn't Sheila. I didn't hear anything on the radio or read anything in the newspapers either. They are keeping a tight lid on this.

Sara Morningsky was a shapeshifter. She could shift into a hawk or a wolf. Even in her human form she could call upon the eyesight of the hawk or scent of the wolf. Her talents came in handy at Dagger Investigations. Whenever Sara shifted into her hawk or wolf form, she and Dagger were able to communicate telepathically. This was something she and her grandmother had been able to do when her grandmother was alive. Sara and Dagger were both surprised that it also worked between the two of them. Dagger thought it had something to do with the black cord necklace with the pendant of a wolf's head Sara's grandmother had given to him.

I'm going to widen the search. The hawk rose on powerful wing beats, then spread its forty-inch wing span, gliding gracefully in an ever-widening circle. Tiny rodents scurried at the sound of the wing beats, burrowing under leaves and scampering across branches. Animals had nothing to fear from this hawk. It wasn't hunting, at least not for four-legged animals.

I don't see anything remotely resembling a human, Dagger, except for the cop out front. Maybe Sheila is still in the house or left with someone. Did you talk to Padre?

No. If it concerns Sheila or her father, I prefer to keep my distance. I suggested that Skizzy check satellite photos, but he said the storm last night made it impossible to see anything. If she left with someone else or was abducted, we have no way of knowing. Her old man hasn't received a ransom call either.

The hawk landed on one of the roof turrets. It cocked its head and studied the figure beneath its talons. *Ugh. Who puts gargoyles on a house anymore?*

Must be a pretty old building. Those were used decades ago to ward off evil spirits.

Well, if anything weird happened in this house last night, the gargoyle wasn't doing its job.

16 The next morning Padre sat at his desk, head in his hands. Chief John Wozniak was seated across from him. "You look like hell," John said.

"Feel like it, too. I got about four hours of sleep last night. Leyton Monroe is going to drive me to an early grave."

"He's just like any father with a missing child."

"No, not like any father. Not every father tries to pull strings to have the FBI brought in, calls in favors from senators to dispatch fifty National Guard to walk a grid through the surrounding forest, nor call the NSA to have them check their satellite feed."

"Has any of it been successful?"

"Satellite photos show zip. Too much storm clutter. The FBI said unless Sheila is on the terrorist watch list, don't bother them. The National Guard would only dispatch ten troops and a pooch or two to do a walk-through sometime this morning. One saving grace is that the state police have cordoned off a five square mile area around the mansion which keeps all the press out of the area."

John balanced a football-sized mug of coffee on his knee. Remnants of a sugar donut could be seen on the knuckles of one hand. "Has Leyton received any calls for a ransom?" He set the mug down and brushed the sugar off of his hand.

"Nothing yet, or at least nothing he has admitted to. Knowing Monroe, if he's ordered not to bring in the police, he won't. Fat chance getting him to take our advice."

"He already broke one cardinal rule. I just heard on the radio that Leyton is offering a hundred thousand dollar reward for information leading to the whereabouts of his daughter."

"Oh, shit." Padre washed his hands over his face. "That will have every idiot calling him with erroneous information, not to mention calls demanding a ransom when they don't have anything whatsoever to do with Sheila's disappearance."

Padre's intercom buzzed prompting a *what now?* expression on his face. He pressed the speaker phone. "Martinez."

"I have a Chase Dagger to see you."

Padre winced. "Damn, I forgot to call him back. Yeah, send him on up."

All work stopped when Sara and Dagger entered the room. Fingers paused on keyboards, phone calls were suspended, voices gradually diminished. Dagger had to fight hard to keep from giving the death ray stares to the men in the room. They paused outside Padre's office. Dagger jammed his hands in the pockets of his cargo pants to keep from pulling his gun. Sometimes it seemed as though Sara was completely oblivious to the effect she had on men. It was as though she looked in the mirror every morning and found flaws where everyone else found perfection.

Padre gave a wave through the glass to come in. John had a big smile for Sara as he assessed her walk, every curve of her body. He knew early on he wouldn't last through the seminary. Three wives later and he was still an outrageous flirt.

"Miss Sara, how nice to see you." John pulled a chair over for her.

"Good morning, Chief, Padre." Sara took a seat, placing her notepad on her lap. They had kept Skizzy's reports at home to avoid explaining to Padre how they obtained the confidential information on Rick Jensen. Sara had Kara's letter and Dagger pretty much memorized what details he felt were important.

John sat on the couch and motioned for Dagger to take the other chair. "I'd ask you if it was okay for me to stay but I'm too plum tired to leave so you'll have to put up with me."

"How is the search going for Sheila?" Dagger asked. "Monroe must be driving everyone crazy."

"You don't know the half of it." John pushed at the air.

"It's a big, damn mystery," Padre said. He leaned back and rocked in his chair. "He's got the National Guard, cadaver dogs, you name it. Then he goes and puts out an award so now we're going to get every idiot in the country calling like they spotted Big Foot."

"We'll make this quick then," Dagger said. "I

received a request from a Kara Jensen regarding her missing husband. He headed for the airport fourteen months ago and never made it to Miami. A Sergeant Miles Vector worked the case."

"I remember him," John said. "Night shift pulled that one. A patrol officer found the car with a flat tire. No driver, no spare, car unlocked. Vector worked that case hard. The man's wife reminded Vector of his own daughter. There was a baby girl from what I recall."

"Bella," Sara offered. "She was six months old when her father disappeared."

"You were on medical leave with a broken ankle, Padre." John tapped the side of his head in a gesture that he hadn't lost any brain cells. "By the time you came back on duty, you were hit hard with that drive-by over on Jackson Place."

"Is anyone assigned to the case now?" Dagger looked from Padre to the chief of detectives.

Wozniak gave a shrug. "I'd have to check whose bottom drawer it's in. I could give it to Spagnola since I don't want him near the Monroe case. Have him dig it out of cold storage."

"No, thanks," Dagger replied. "I'd sooner have a lobotomy than talk to that idiot."

"Still bad blood between you two?" Padre made a tsking sound. "Thought you were over Sheila."

"I am. Just don't like Spagnola's attitude. If you remember, Padre, he tends to use his fists when interrogating."

John snapped his gaze to Padre. "What's this?"

Padre waved off the question. "Fill you in later." It was during the Friday the Thirteenth case that Joe had hauled Dagger in for questioning since Dagger had a key to Sheila's condo and someone had gained access and killed Sheila's assistant. It was speculated that the killer's target had been Sheila. Since Sheila and Dagger had not had a friendly breakup, Joe kept Dagger on ice while the real killer was still out there, his sights turned to Sara.

Padre pecked at the keyboard and brought up the Jensen file. "Very cold trail on this one. Media speculated Jensen might have taken off with a new squeeze."

John asked, "Have you spoken with the wife?"

"We wanted to get an update from your department first," Dagger replied.

"According to her letter, Kara swears they had a solid marriage and, besides, Rick would never have left Bella. She was his world." Sara pulled out a wedding photo of the happy couple.

John heaved himself off the couch and leaned over Padre's shoulder. "Looks like my wedding photo, all three of them. We all look happy on that day, then it's downhill from there."

Sara handed them a photo of Bella, her eyes bright and smiling, a pink band in her hair.

"She is a cutie," Padre agreed.

"Rick even went so far as to get a tattoo with Bella's name on the rim of a bell." Sara showed them a photo of Rick in a sleeveless tee shirt, his arm turned toward the camera.

Padre's jaw went slack. John grabbed the photo and

stared. "When did he disappear?"

"Fourteen months ago," Dagger said. "Why?"

"Can't be," Padre said. "Our vic just died and his tattoo is fresh, certainly not fourteen months old."

"What are you talking about?" Dagger asked.

"I don't understand," Sara chimed in.

Padre said, "Want to take a trip to the morgue?"

17 Padre handed Luther the case file on Rick Jensen. "We may have identified your John Doe."

Dagger wasn't concerned or shocked that seeing a dead body didn't bother Sara. Padre and John, on the other hand, weren't sure she should be there, concerned that at her young age of nineteen she wouldn't be able to handle a body much less the odor of the morgue. But Sara strode right up to the gurney and studied John Doe as though he were a patient with a rash.

"He does have a resemblance to Rick Jensen but how could that be? This man just died." Sara almost bumped heads with Dagger as she moved closer to the tattoo. "That does look fresh, right?"

"Looks as though it was just done twenty-four hours ago," Dagger said. "Maybe he had it redone. Is that possible?"

"If it were possible," Luther said, "we would see some underlying evidence of the previous tattoo. No tattoo artist is that good that he can literally replicate every stroke of the previous tat."

"So this guy was found on the Sebold property strangled with a scarf?" Dagger asked.

"Oh, that ain't the best part," Padre said with a

chuckle. "The scarf belonged to Sheila."

"We need proof," John said. "We need to compare John Doe's fingerprints with Rick Jensen's. Anything in the case file, Luther? Like sample prints, hair off of a hair brush?"

Luther held up one finger while he read from the file. "Evidence box should have hair samples and fingerprints. Missus Jensen had submitted a plaster of her husband's hand. It was a wall hanging of all three hands when Bella was born. Forensics made a mold of his print so that should confirm the identity of our John Doe." His finger tapped one of the entries. He picked up his current autopsy report on John Doe. "This is interesting. Fourteen months ago Kara Jensen reported that her husband left for the airport after eating scrambled eggs, a cinnamon roll, and drinking three cups of coffee." He nodded at the body of John Doe. "The stomach contents of our friend here consisted of coffee, eggs, and a cinnamon roll consumed roughly one hour before his death."

18

"I haven't been in this thick of brush since I was a kid on my family's ranch in Oklahoma."

Mike Reynolds carved his way through the weeds, his heavy boots crushing dried stalks and leaves before sinking into the soggy earth. His trained eyes were looking for cleared areas, mounds of overturned dirt. Anything that would give them a hint that a body had recently been buried.

"Weren't you ever a boy scout?" Abe Galto was ten feet away, eyes on the cadaver dogs shuffling through the brush. "We could clear an acre in less than a day using only our pocketknives."

Mike studied his fellow guardsmen dotting the landscape with brown camouflage outfits. Abe was the oldest and his responses were always prefaced by words that sounded like, "back in my day." Compared to Mike and the other eight National Guardsmen, Abe was a dinosaur, preferring to never rise in rank. The younger guys didn't think it was because Abe wasn't worthy of a stripe or two. They felt it was because he wanted to spout off his years of experience to the young pups. To his credit, Abe was still fit and active, despite the graying hair and sagging chest.

"Pocketknife, right," Mike said with a shake of his head. "You probably set the damn acre on fire and stood there with a water hose."

"Yep, back then," Abe continued, ignoring Mike's comment, "we weren't soft the way kids are today. We could work from sun up to sun down without one word of complaint."

Mike had to agree with him there. Even his own son who was eight would rather lie on the couch and play video games than chase a baseball with the neighborhood boys. They were raising a generation of couch potatoes.

Abe looked back at the sprawling mansion. "Can you believe how the rich lived? Probably entertained royalty and a few shady characters, you know, like Capone." Abe still lived the past, not just in his thinking but also in his appearance. His hair was kept in a short brush cut, the same as his college yearbook picture. His street clothes were something out of a sixties Sears catalog. And the younger men salivated over his 1968 Ford Fairlane which had less than twenty thousand miles on the odometer.

"Back when I was growing up we lived in a brick bungalow with one bedroom and one bathroom. Me and my two brothers slept upstairs in the attic which was converted into two bedrooms. We had two inches of ice on the inside of the windows in the winter. Two inches. And we didn't have air conditioning."

"It's a wonder you survived." Mike shoved his boot against a boulder, flipping it over which disturbed a family of multi-legged insects. Abe continued as though he hadn't heard Mike's rhetorical jab.

"My dad provided for a family of five on ten thousand dollars a year. But look at that house. Bet it takes that much just to pay the monthly electric bill."

One of the dogs started scratching at the ground, sniffing, scratching some more, then laid down. Another dog started to bark an alarm and then the boots started pounding toward the area.

They moved quickly to where the lead dog lay. Colonel Tom Hegner held his arms out to keep the men back. He knelt down and patted the German shepherd on the head. "What did you find, Abby?" Two guardsmen approached with shovels while the colonel took a gloved hand and raked away leaves and dead weeds with his fingers to reveal a square slab of concrete.

They were gathered now, all ten guardsmen surrounding the colonel and cadaver dogs. "Well, Abe," Mike said. "In your day, what significance was a square piece of concrete?"

"It's probably a cover to an old well. Since this is unincorporated area, I doubt they were hooked up to city water. However, with a mansion this size, I doubt the owners had to carry water from a well. Place has electricity and all the other modern conveniences. The well probably hasn't been used in decades. Might have been dug and never used."

Colonel Hegner said, "Let's see if it will pry off. According to Abby, there's something here."

They didn't need the shovels to pry off the lid, just four strong men to lift and move it to the side. The well was six feet across, the walls lined with brick. Several of the men stepped back, expecting the scent of decomposing flesh, but all that escaped was a musty, moldy odor.

Hegner leaned over the edge. It was too deep to see the bottom. "Let's get a light down there."

Within five minutes, one young guardsman was suited up like a rock climber. Hegner checked the guard's helmet, turning on the miner's light in the front. "Your mike working, Biejewski?"

"Testing one, two, three." Biejewski was slight in build yet quick and agile as a crab when it came to climbing.

Hegner checked his own earpiece. "Coming in loud and clear." The colonel shook his head as Biejewski hooked the rope onto the side of the well, gave it a few tugs to make sure it held, then started down. "Bebe. Young, dumb, and fearless," Hegner said under his breath. In his youth Hegner probably would have been just as daring.

Hegner heard Bebe's voice in his earpiece. "Pretty slimy walls. Mold, multi-legged creatures. I've descended about thirty feet so far. No sign of scraping on the sides to indicate anyone or anything had been tossed down here recently."

Hegner wasn't above asking Abe's opinion. After all, Abe was at least fifteen years his senior. "Abe, what's the water table in this area?"

"I'd say they'd have to go down a minimum of one hundred feet to hit water." Abe leaned over and peered down into the vast cavern. "Hope it isn't two hundred feet or Bebe would have had to pack a lunch. In my day..." Everyone groaned.

"I can see bottom, I think, Sarge," Biejewski yelled. "I've gone down a little over one hundred fifty feet."

The men jockeyed for a view. They were of all ages and backgrounds. Almost all of them had been deployed to the Gulf region during the BP oil spill last year.

"Would be nice if we had a camera on his helmet," Mike said.

"Oh, jeez." Bebe's voice sounded strained in Hegner's earpiece.

"Did you find a body, Bebe?" Hegner asked.

"No, Colonel," Bebe replied. After a pause he added, "I found two."

19 Padre rushed from the car to the back of the mansion. The fast food hamburger he had rammed down his throat on the drive over was burning a hole in his stomach. It had been twenty-five hours since the Monroes had reported their daughter missing. As he approached he saw two National Guard trucks parked in an area one hundred yards from the mansion. Guardsmen and police officers were huddled around what Padre could assume was the well where the bodies were found. The area looked as though someone had taken a machete to the overgrowth. Overhead the overcast skies gave little hint as to when it planned to dump its next rainfall.

Parked nearby was the medical examiner's van. Luther was climbing into a jump suit of some type. Padre couldn't believe Luther was contemplating going down into the well. Since what were found were skeletal remains, Padre saw no reason to contact Leyton Monroe.

"Aren't you getting a little old for cliff climbing, Luther?"

"Nah. Besides, I'm going down, not up."

A sophisticated pulley system stretched across the opening to the well, supported on either side by National Guard vehicles. One of the guardsmen tested the pulley while another helped Luther into a harness. The men in camouflage were a mixture of middle-aged office workers who had added a few pounds over the years to young studs who looked as though they spent eight hours every day in the gym.

One rather large, muscular black man wore his sunglasses on the top of his bald head. Dog tags hung around his neck and his biceps looked larger than Padre's thighs. He appeared to be the man in charge.

"Are you Colonel Hegner?" Padre thrust a hand toward the large man who sported a tan tee shirt. "Sergeant Padre Martinez. You can call me Padre."

"Guess it's a good thing we didn't find your missing woman. Leaves hope she might still be alive."

Padre peered into the dark well, then shook his head at the medical examiner. "You're really going down there?" He had firsthand knowledge that Luther was a bit of a daredevil. Padre had discovered that when hanging onto the back of Luther's motorcycle while it careened down a gravel road into a quarry. "So there're two skeletons down there."

"So I'm told."

Padre eyed the equipment hanging from Luther's belt. There were two toaster-sized flashlights, a video cam, and a modified evidence kit. His helmet was equipped with a miner's light and a camera. Finally, he shrugged into a backpack. It looked to Padre like all the equipment weighed more than Luther.

"Are you going to stay for the show?" Hegner asked Padre. "I hear this house has all kinds of secrets."

"That it does."

Two guardsmen helped Luther to the edge of the well. They hooked him up and slowly lowered him. Luther gave a thumbs up and ignored Padre when he made a sign of the cross.

Padre stepped to the back of one of the trucks where a computer monitor rested on a tailgate. "Got some fancy equipment here," he told Hegner.

"We have training exercises in caves. Never know when it might come in handy." Hegner tapped several keys on the keyboard. "Luckily your medical examiner brought his own computer monitor. With the video cam we can see and record everything he is seeing. And there's a microphone here if you want to talk to him."

Two of Luther's assistants hauled stretchers from the back of the van and carried them to the side of the well.

"How are you doing, Doc?" Padre asked. On the monitor Padre could see the brick walls of the well. Some type of algae coated the sides and eight or more legged beasts were scurrying away from the light. "Please don't bring any of your friends back with you."

"There's like nothing to touch," Luther reported. "There are slimy things everywhere. The well looks about six foot wide. Shouldn't be too difficult getting those stretchers down here. With all the rain we've had lately, it appears to have saturated the ground. Makes the bricks look like they are bleeding."

"Thanks for the visual, Doc."

The further down he descended, the dryer and less damp were the walls. Portions of the wall had crumbled from age. The light beam lit up the bottom of the dry well as Luther hovered overhead, angling for a spot to place his feet without stepping on the deceased. "I have reached bottom. Have you got visuals on your end?"

"Yes, Doctor Jamison. We hear you loud and clear," Colonel Hegner said. "And it is recording so go ahead and give us your assessment."

Luther detached the flashlights from his belt. From a backpack he removed metal legs, which, when extended, became a tripod in which to fasten each light. After setting one on each side, he squatted down to first examine the soil.

"The ground is bone dry." Luther pointed for the benefit of the camera. "There is evidence of copious amount of fly pupae cases."

"That far down?" Padre asked.

"Sure. They have been found in Indian burial grounds dating back three thousand years." He used tweezers to place several of the pupae cases in a plastic container. He snapped on a lid and placed the container in his backpack. On the monitor the camera panned the skeletons. They were clothed in fabric that had long since started to deteriorate. He pulled out his own camera and took digital snapshots on the off chance anything disrupted the computer recordings. Next he carefully peeled away the clothing and studied the ribs, pelvic area, tibias, and then the skull. "We have one female and one male. I would estimate their age at death between forty and fifty years of age. Difficult to tell height without measuring the bones." With gloved hands he carefully lifted just the corners of the fabric to search under the bodies but the fabric started to disintegrate in his hands. "I don't see a weapon but it could be under their bodies. Have to wait until my assistant removes the bodies to get a better look. Clothes are definitely from another period, maybe early nineteen hundreds." Luther lifted the collar of the man's shirt. Puzzled, he did the same with the high collar of the woman's dress. "I do see some type of rope under the victims. They could have been hung or perhaps restrained before being thrown down the well."

Padre felt a drop of water on his hand and looked up at the sky. "We're going to have to erect a tent over the opening, Doc. We've got a light rain starting up."

"Connor, Miller," Hegner yelled at two men near one of the trucks. "We need a canopy constructed over the well." Hegner turned back to the monitor and said, "Maybe the house was part of the underground railroad and they had been helping to free some slaves," he suggested. "Or maybe they were slaves."

"No, these two are Caucasian," Luther replied.

As several guardsmen hurried to erect a canopy over the well, Padre snapped open his own umbrella. A strange thought came to mind as he watched the gentle drizzle touch the earth. It was as though Nature herself were weeping.

20

Luther walked into Padre's office, the odor of pasta wafting through the air. Padre and John were hovered over plates of spaghetti. John pointed over his shoulder at a counter against the wall. "Wife brought it in. It's in the crock pot, still hot. Plates are in the cabinet."

"Smells good," Luther said as he tapped an envelope against his thigh. "But I have dinner waiting on the stove at home." He leaned against the credenza careful not to knock over the display of family photos. Padre opened a bottom desk drawer and held up a bottle of scotch but Luther waved him off. "How did Kara Jensen take the news about her husband?"

"As well as can be expected. She had never given up hope," Padre said with a sigh. "Course, I didn't mention the tattoo or the last meal he ate. She's going to be in tomorrow with her father. She wants to see her husband's body."

Luther pulled glossy photos from an envelope. "This you are going to love."

Padre shook his head. "Nothing is going to spoil this fabulous authentic Italian meal. Besides, I don't think we can take any more surprises."

Luther's smile was a little too devilish and a sign

that he was enjoying giving them more gray hairs. He handed them a photo of a close-up of Rick Jensen's neck. It showed different angles, front, side, back and one photo close enough to see the detail of the knot and bow tied at the back. If Luther's smile got any wider, his face would split in two.

"Okay, what's the punch line?" John asked. "We've seen this before."

"The two victims in the well, which I am ruling as homicides, and who I'm estimating were murdered at least seventy-five or more years ago, and..." He paused at this point as his gaze shifted to each of the men. "Experts inform me that there are all indications no one has disturbed the concrete lid on that well in as many years." He set several more photos on the desk. "The rope found in the well was actually two pieces of rope, each tied around one of the victims. My assistant and I tried to carefully remove the rope but it is so old it literally disintegrated in our hands. Got good pictures though before it was destroyed." Luther pointed at another photo. "As you can tell, those ropes were tied in a bow." Padre and John locked gazes, then snapped back to the photos.

Luther continued. "Now, some people tie bows left to right, some right to left. Some loop over, some under. I've tried every scenario possible but my conclusions are accurate. I would stake my reputation on it." The two men waited, eyebrows raised, forks hovering. They never knew Luther to go for the melodramatic. "Rick Jensen and the two victims in the well were killed the identical way." Luther watched spaghetti noodles drift off their forks and splatter to the plate. "I'll have that drink now."

Padre and John didn't speak for several minutes as Padre filled paper cups of scotch and passed them around. Their plates of spaghetti were left untouched. "This has to be wrong, that's the only logical conclusion. It's a prank," Padre surmised. "Whoever killed Jensen somehow found the well and thought it would be clever to make it look like the same person has been around for what? One hundred years? You know that's completely impossible for it to be the same person. Right?"

"Padre, he said the lid to the well hasn't been opened in just as many years," John reminded him. "There isn't any way you can duplicate that."

"And don't forget," Luther reminded them, "that Rick Jensen was dressed in the same clothes he left the house in fourteen months ago and had the identical meal in his stomach." He tossed a folder on the desk as though it were the final straw. "If you want my opinion, someone needs to spend a night in that house. Miss Monroe disappears. A dead body shows up like he just left home yesterday, and then you find two bodies killed the same way over seventy-five years ago. There is definitely something strange going on." Luther studied the liquid in his glass and raised it for a toast. "I only know of one person who is an expert at strange."

Padre gave that comment a very brief consideration before looking at John. Then they both slowly smiled.

21 Dagger slid his eyes to Sara. The last thing he wanted to do was get involved in anything to do with Sheila. Sara on the other hand had the gleam of excitement in her eyes. He could tell by the smile she was trying desperately to rein in that she was fascinated by the case. Dagger had told Padre "no, under no uncertain terms," when he had called last night about the Sebold mansion. Dagger didn't doubt for one second that Sheila had taken off to New York or Paris on an impulse. Nor did he doubt that she would stoop to the lowest depths to put herself in some questionable danger just to see if he would ride off to the rescue.

Chief Wozniak set another cup of coffee in front of Dagger. Being pampered by the chief of detectives set Dagger's radar quaking. What exactly did this case involve that even Wozniak was eager to engage Dagger's help? Two additional chairs had been dragged into the compact office. As if Wozniak's hostessing efforts weren't suspicion enough, Padre was wearing the shell-shocked face of someone in the final throes of desperation.

Dagger rubbed the fatigue from his eyes. He had never been one to sleep past six in the morning, not until Nebraska. Whether it was because his body needed more healing or the disturbing dreams kept him from sleeping soundly, he was more inclined to wake at the crack of nine. Sara's insistence that they hear Padre out was the only reason he was sitting in Padre's office at eight o'clock.

Padre checked his watch. Dagger knew who entered the room even before he turned around. The smell of stale cigar smoke preceded the portly patriarch of a publishing empire.

"You have got to be kidding," Leyton bellowed. "This idiot probably kidnapped my daughter and stashed her somewhere just to get the reward money." He wedged himself into one of the arm chairs offered by John.

Dagger tossed a steely glare at Leyton. How like him to have the entire police department chasing their tails looking for his daughter. If it were a son or daughter of a family from the poverty stricken side of town, he doubted law enforcement agencies would be this inclined to move heaven and earth.

"I'm not interested. Your spoiled brat of a daughter is probably shopping in Paris." But his words were clipped short by the intense pain radiating from his forearm where Sara had clamped a vice grip. He tried not to wince at the pain. Sometimes Sara didn't realize her own strength.

"How much is the reward?" she asked Leyton.

Leyton shifted his gaze from Dagger to Sara. "One hundred thousand."

"We'll take one-fifty."

"What?" was on the tip of Dagger's lips but Sara drilled him with her ice blues. He pried her fingers loose, much to the amusement of Padre, and struggled to keep the sweat from forming on his forehead. There was something about this case that truly excited Sara. Money was never a priority in Sara's life. No. She was probably doing this for him, getting him interested in working cases again.

"See." Leyton jammed a chubby finger at Dagger. "He's guilty. I would sooner look for my daughter myself than pay this hoodlum one dime."

"Leyton." John bit back a retort. He and Padre were still trying to digest the details Luther had dumped in their laps last night. "We've tried every normal, logical approach to finding your daughter and we've come up empty. Why not give him a shot? What have you got to lose?"

"He's got a point," Padre added. "If search dogs and all the manpower we have expended haven't turned her up, all we can assume is she's on a shopping spree in New York. And if that's the case, we will see to it she is prosecuted for wasting our time."

"Don't forget, we do have a body with her scarf around his neck. How do we know she didn't kill him and is on the run?" John added. "If anything, you are trusting Dagger to prove your daughter's innocence. That should be worth something."

Monroe swiped chubby fingers across his mouth. His eyes seethed pure hatred at the P.I. "All right," he finally replied. "But I'm not paying one dime over the stated reward of one hundred thousand."

Sara's eyes silently pleaded and Dagger was a sucker for those eyes. "All right, I'll settle for the original reward on one condition. If it is determined that she is playing all of us, you will donate one hundred and fifty thousand to a charity of my choosing."

Leyton mumbled something that sounded like he agreed, then stared at the rug as he charged out of the office and toward the elevators.

Dagger reached over and shoved the door closed. "Okay, now that you have us here, spill the rest of the story."

"We have positively identified John Doe as Rick Jensen," Padre started. "He disappeared fourteen months ago. On the original missing person report, Missus Jensen knew exactly what her husband was wearing and what he had to eat. He was wearing the exact same clothes when we found him and Luther found the identical contents in the vic's stomach. The wife also claims his tattoo was fresh, just two days old. John Doe's tattoo was fresh."

"Tell me something we don't know." Dagger grabbed his cup of coffee. Damn, the chief even gave him a saucer.

"Tell them the rest," John told Padre.

"There's more?" Sara couldn't be more excited if she were sitting in a cemetery. What on earth had he created? Dagger wondered.

"There's an old well on the premises containing two skeletons. Luther estimates they have been dead for over eighty years. They were strangled with a rope tied the exact way as the scarf found around Rick Jensen's neck."

"Really?" Sara smiled. "How cool is that? I mean, not for them of course. Were they the previous owners?"

"We haven't identified them yet," Padre replied.

"What about these ghost hunters? Anything in their background? Any problems reported on their previous hunts?" Dagger had to smile at his own choice of words.

"When I first heard about the case...no evidence, no clues... the first thought that came to mind was human trafficking. Sheila could be on a cargo ship set for the Middle East somewhere. Have these ghost hunters been checked out as far as people missing from other cities where they have been?"

"Nothing," Padre replied. "They have only been in business a couple years. People who have hired them in the past haven't had any complaints. No crimes were committed before. Even passed a lie detector test, but just the thought of what they do is creepy enough."

"It's all studio manufactured, if you listen to Leyton," John interjected. "Sheila's whole reason for agreeing to participate was to expose them as frauds. Maybe she found something out and they couldn't have her reporting it. It would ruin them. Leyton believes they did something with his daughter."

"I think we should have them with us," Sara suggested. "We can keep an eye on them, they might slip up, especially if they had anything to do with Sheila's disappearance."

"Do you think just two of you can keep an eye on three people?" Padre asked.

"Sure? Why not?" although Dagger was starting to wonder about the size of this mansion.

"Padre has a point." Chief Wozniak turned to his sergeant. "Which is why you're joining them."

"Me? You are not serious." Padre instinctively reached for the crucifix tucked under his shirt.

22 Sheila tapped her watch. "I don't understand. I just had the battery changed a couple months ago."

"It doesn't work here," Colleen said.

"Why not?"

Her tiny shoulders shrugged. "Nothing works here." Colleen propped her doll on her lap. It had the same pinafore dress that Colleen wore.

Sheila walked over to the window and studied the endless acres of trees and wildflowers. "Where are your power lines?"

"What are those?"

"You know, electricity to run the refrigerator, microwave, lights." Sheila pointed to a lamp on the desk, but then realized it was a kerosene lantern. On a table against the wall was an old time Victrola which had to be cranked to work. Where had she seen one of those recently? "Of course!" Sheila exclaimed. "That's it!"

"What's it?" Colleen set the doll next to her as Sheila returned to the couch. "That's why the name Dawson's Corner sounds familiar. I researched the history for an article I was writing about the one hundred anniversary of Cedar Point. I interviewed dozens of people and spent hours at the Historical Society going through all of their books and studying their display cases. Cedar Point was first known as Dawson's Corner. And that's why, oh god." Tears sprang to her eyes.

"Why are you crying?" Colleen's angelic face showed concern and fear.

"They are happy tears, sweetheart. I now know where I'm at. I'm in a coma and I'm dreaming everything. That's why I'm in this turn of the century house without modern conveniences and why you don't know about iPhones and iPads, computers, electricity. And the name. I remember the people who used to live here, the man who started the harbor. Sebold… husband and wife." Sheila was spitting out details faster than her mind could keep up. Everything was coming back to her and she suddenly wondered if her parents were standing vigil by her bedside. Could she feel her mother holding her hand, patting her forehead with a cool cloth? The fact that she was remembering her research should be a sign that she was recovering. "Wait. I remember the name Walker, too. Not Adrian. No." Sheila searched her memory then snapped her fingers. "Leeland! Yes, that's it."

"What is it about my father?" Adrian appeared in the doorway like a specter. He rarely made a sound except when he was coming down the creaky staircase. Immediately Colleen's eyes widened and she scooted closer to Sheila.

"Why is she afraid of you? If you have hurt her in any way." Sheila wrapped a protective arm around the girl.

Walker moved like a cat, languid and deliberate, and squatted down in front of Colleen. "I would never hurt her.

She's my sister."

"That's impossible," Sheila said. "You have to be at least forty years older than her. Is she adopted?" Sheila turned Colleen's face toward her. "You can tell me the truth, honey. Is he your brother?"

Colleen shook her head yes. Obviously they had different fathers, Sheila surmised.

"And has he ever harmed you in anyway?"

Slowly Colleen shook her head no, but she cast her eyes down, refusing to look at Walker. She moved closer to Sheila and whispered, "But he's hurt other people."

"Now Colleen. What have I told you about telling secrets? Be truthful, little one. If you want to tell her about harmful people, you should tell her about mother."

With that one word Colleen stiffened. Sheila had seen fear in Colleen's eyes when she had heard Walker descending the stairs but this was different. Her eyes held terror. But if Walker were close to fifty, how old were the parents? Were they still alive?

"What on earth did she do that would make this child so fearful?"

"Doesn't matter any more. She's dead." Walker straightened but kept his eyes on Colleen. "Miss Monroe and I are going to talk. Would you take your doll upstairs?"

Colleen looked out of the window at the sky and shook her head no. "It's coming."

"What's coming?" Sheila hated the cryptic conversation between these two."

"Colleen is afraid of thunderstorms."

"I was, too, when I was your age. It's always more

comforting to be with other people."

Colleen shook her head no and looked out the window again. Adrian clasped her small hands between his. She didn't pull away. "Okay then. You can stay down here but Miss Monroe and I are going to talk big people talk. How about if you take your doll to the dining room?"

"We'll be right here," Sheila assured her. Colleen stared at her with big blue eyes. Sheila brushed stray hairs from Colleen's face. "We'll just be a few steps away." Colleen nodded and left the room.

Adrian took a seat at the other end of the couch. Sheila edged back on her end and turned to face him. "Tell me about yourself, Mr. Walker."

"Please call me Adrian."

"Fine, Adrian." She wished she had her notepad with her but why should anyone in a coma write notes? "How old are you?"

Walker dismissed the question with a wave of his hand. "Age is inconsequential."

"How long have you lived here?"

Walker stared at the ceiling for several seconds but Sheila knew a stall when she saw one. Finally he replied with a smile, "All of my life. But truly, I want to find out more about modern technology and this Internet you talk about and how one can take pictures with a phone. I know about electricity and the dial telephones, although my parents couldn't afford either."

"I can tell you about them but not how they work. I'm not an expert on electronics. You do know about cars."

Adrian nodded. "I've never owned one but I have

heard about them."

"Well, there is a small gadget about the size of a box of matches that when you press a button you can unlock the doors by remote, you can even start it by remote. There are remote garage door openers, robots that vacuum your house. And even cell phones can set your security alarm on your house and even unlock car doors."

Adrian looked fascinated. "Do go on."

So Sheila told him about traffic cameras, GPS, satellites, the Hubble telescope, nuclear power, laptops and notepads, trips to the moon, the Discovery shuttle, wars, one hundred story buildings, flat screen television sets, microwave ovens, CDs and DVDs, wind power, solar power. But for all his total interest in what she had to say, his only question baffled her.

"Who is your most famous killer?"

"What?" Sheila shook her head as though not hearing correctly. Suddenly something about the name Walker nagged at the back of her memory. "What do you mean?"

"You still have crime don't you?"

"Of course. There are robberies, drive-by shootings. Humans still find ways to inflict pain on other humans." There was something strange in Adrian's eyes when he talked about murder. Sheila couldn't put her finger on it. She had seen the same look in the eyes of a pit bull when she had written a story about dog fights. Walker... where had she read about a killer named Walker? "What technology do you remember and what kind of music and movies do you like?" Sheila wanted to get him off the subject of murder.

"Casablanca. I so loved that movie." Adrian relaxed a bit and sat back with a smile. "Gary Cooper and Humphrey Bogart are fabulous actors."

"They are dead." Sheila blurted it out before she could catch herself. Adrian looked crestfallen.

"How dreadful. When?"

"Sorry. I keep forgetting that I live in the year 2011." The look on Adrian's face reminded her that she had not mentioned the current year before.

"Good Lord," Adrian whispered. "Judy Garland? Jimmy Stewart? Elizabeth Taylor?"

Sheila winced. "Sorry." That didn't seem to make him feel better. "Price of gas is over three dollars a gallon."

"Preposterous! How does anyone afford to drive?"

"What else do you remember?"

"Those who owned television sets had a choice of thirteen channels."

"Over two and sometimes three hundred stations on satellite TV," Sheila countered.

"Ten cents a pack for cigarettes."

"Over fifty dollars a carton now."

"Really? Good lord. I'm glad I don't smoke."

Now that she had him off the subject of the crime rate, Adrian was much more animated, had a gentle, rather attractive smile. This Adrian she could become accustomed to.

"The Carrolls in town bought a car for fifteen hundred."

"Four tires for my car cost fifteen hundred."

They laughed, loud enough to make Colleen peek

around the corner from the dining room.

"How about a tour of the house as you had requested earlier?" Adrian suggested.

Some lines never changed through the years. When a man wanted to give you a tour of his humble abode, it usually meant his bedroom. But Sheila was in a coma and it wouldn't be the first time she had sex in her sleep. She grabbed his hand and stood but the room started to swim and her stomach lurched. Sheila slowly lowered herself back down.

"I don't think climbing stairs sounds like a very good idea just yet."

Adrian gave a nod of his head. "Maybe later. I do so enjoy your company." He reached over, grabbed her hand and kissed it. There was something in his touch that was too soft, too insincere, and too cold.

23

"Let me get this straight." Skizzy had a way of jerking his eyebrows in two different directions. With both eyes wobbling in their sockets, it made for a comical impression. "Some ghost hunters spent the night in a haunted mansion, the rich lady disappeared, a body shows up out of nowhere with her scarf around his neck, the guy is wearing the same clothes and fresh tattoo he sported when he left fourteen months ago. Then two ancient skeletons are found in a well with rope around their necks tied the exact same way as the current victim. Now you have been hired to spend the night in the mansion to see if you can figure out if the ghost hunters are guilty of any of the happenings at the mansion." Skizzy huffed and scratched at his torn tee shirt. "Someone's yanking someone's chain. As far as the rich bitch, I'd say she's with all the other people who have been reported missing over the years."

Dagger refused to bite but before he could warn Sara, she said, "And where's that?"

"Why, kidnapped by aliens. Where do you think, girlie?"

Sara's withering look at Dagger told him *thanks for the warning.*

Skizzy leaned his elbows on the counter and lowered

his voice to a conspiratorial level. "Have you ever heard a ringing in your ears? The pitch is low at first and then gets real loud. That's the aliens downloading directions to you to be at a certain place at a certain time. Some people, their brains can't decipher the alien language and just ignore them. But others go off like good little Stepford boys and girls, right to the meeting place where..." Skizzy clapped his hands together so fast and loud Sara's body jerked. "Bam, that beam of light shoots down and sucks them right up."

Skizzy disappeared into the back room. Dagger rubbed his forearm where Sara had dug in her nails. "It's a good thing I heal quickly."

"I wasn't about ready to let this case slip through our fingers. Besides, watching you mope around all day is very depressing. It isn't healthy for you to stay secluded."

The concern in her eyes pulled at his black heart strings. It seemed like ages ago that she had walked into his office wearing what resembled a handmade sack dress. She had looked like a street urchin begging for a handout. How wrong he had been. Now she shops at Christopher & Banks and developed a penchant for anything floral. She didn't as much wear the clothes as they adapted to her. Gone were those shaky steps in her first pair of heels. And gone was her fear of him. What she probably would never outgrow was her fear of crowds. Quite understandable considering how her parents had died.

Skizzy emerged from the backroom and set a laptop on the counter followed by battery packs. He disappeared into his hidey-hole again.

"I think we need to stop at Subway and pick up some sandwiches, maybe pack a cooler with bottles of water, cans of soda," Sara suggested. "We'll need some ammo, just in case the ghosts are human."

"I can deal with the human kind. Don't know what we will need for the other kind."

"Padre will probably bring the holy water," Sara said with a laugh.

Skizzy returned and added two oblong silver cases to the collection on the counter, and something Dagger could swear was a geiger counter.

"Hold up. I don't have time to learn how all this stuff works."

"I know." Skizzy smiled revealing a mouth of mismatched teeth. "Which is why I'm going with you."

Skizzy and a house of roving ghosts. Dagger didn't know which scared him more.

"How are we going to handle this?" Chief Wozniak asked Padre. "We can't tell the widow that his tattoo is fresh. Hopefully, she won't notice. And we can't give her his clothes back. She might recognize that they are the same clothes he wore when he left fourteen months ago."

"Definitely not. I'll just tell her Forensics has his clothes. They will be cutting them up, processing them. There won't be much to give back. I'll just give her his watch. We didn't find a wallet on him. And with any luck she won't notice that the tattoo is still fresh. We can dance around that subject, tell her Forensics had to put some oil or something on it to make an impression which is why it looks so fresh."

John tapped the watch. "Uh, I don't think we can give her the watch."

"Why's that?"

"It stopped on the date that her husband disappeared."

Wozniak saw a figure approaching from down the hall. She was attractive in a country girl sort of way. A short, no-fuss hair cut, framed a heart-shaped face. "Here she comes."

Padre met Kara partway. Her eyes were red and swollen and she clutched her purse like a life vest. Padre clasped both of her hands in his. "Our heartfelt apologizes for your loss. I know this is devastating for you. Is someone watching your little girl?"

"My parents drove in from Indianapolis. Bella is with my mom. My dad is parking the car."

"That's good. You should have someone with you when you identify the body."

A tall man in a suit appeared in the doorway. He patted stray hairs as he hustled down the corridor. Padre introduced himself and Wozniak. Lee Atwater shook each of their hands firmly, then wrapped an arm around his daughter. His face was a mask of sorrow as he kissed Kara on the side of her head.

"What a horrible thing to happen, Sergeant. Kara's mother and I were so critical of Rick at the beginning, thinking that he had up and left our daughter and granddaughter. Then to have this happen. Do you have any idea where Rick has been all this time?"

"We are still trying to piece together the last fourteen months. The fact that he didn't have identification on him could signify robbery and assault. It's possible he had amnesia. We just won't know until we get his photo out to the other cities to see if anyone recognizes him."

"When will the body be released so we can make arrangements?" Lee asked.

Kara clung to him tightly, a hankie pressed to her face.

"I should know something from the medical examiner tomorrow."

One of Luther's assistants opened a door and poked his head out. He nodded toward Padre. "They are ready." Padre accompanied them into the room and watched as an assistant in blue scrubs pulled back the sheet. Kara let out a sob and buried her face in her father's shoulder.

"It's him," Lee said. "It's Rick."

Lucky for Padre, Kara did not ask to have the sheet brought down past Rick's head.

"Where was he found?" Lee asked.

Padre looked at Wozniak. The chief replied, "In an unincorporated area outside of town. It will take awhile to track his whereabouts for the past fourteen months. We will first send his picture out to area hospitals and then widen the search."

"Why hospitals?" Kara asked behind her hankie.

"Our medical examiner found an old head wound so it's possible he had amnesia after being assaulted," Wozniak replied while Padre's eyes flicked toward the ceiling as though praying for John's lying soul. "He may have been in a hospital."

"But wouldn't the hospital have put his photo in the paper or sent it out to the police departments?" Lee Atwater was going to make Padre and Wozniak dance a jig before the day was over.

"It may not have been a hospital in this state. And there's a possibility it was a kidnapping and after several months he got away but still didn't know who he was."

Padre decided John was pretty good at dancing a jig, and a polka and any two step or side step.

This only made Kara cry harder. "We'll never know what horrors he had to go through."

Wozniak led them away from the morgue. "We'll keep you apprised of anything we discover concerning the case. You have my word on it."

"What about his watch?" Kara sniffed. "I gave it to him on our first anniversary."

The chief shook his head with genuine remorse. "Sorry. The thief must have taken that, too."

Padre again sought forgiveness from the man upstairs.

Part Two

*The distinction between the past, present and future
is only a stubbornly persistent illusion*

Albert Einstein
(1879-1955)

24

Dagger stopped the Lincoln Navigator about fifty yards in from the street. He and Sara both slowly climbed out and, leaving the doors open, just stood and gawked at the massive structure one hundred yards in front of them.

"Wow," was all Sara could say. The building looked four stories high, not two as Padre had said. The roof of the veranda rested on six marble columns while the rest of the structure was dark stone reaching up to castle-like turrets. "It's as though the owner didn't know if he wanted a plantation or gothic mansion. All that's missing are the moat and drawbridge."

"Look at those damn gargoyles. I should use them for target practice." The beasts eyed them suspiciously. It didn't help that dark clouds appeared to rest on the gargoyles' shoulders. "Kids are usually warned against trick or treating at houses that looked like this." He glanced over the hood of the Navigator at his partner. Sara's eyes looked like a kid's on Christmas morning. But there was something else that was happening. As she turned her head he could see that Sara had called on the vision of the hawk and was carefully scrutinizing the house. A hawk's vision was eight times the acuity of a human's. Exactly what she was looking for he didn't know. "Any ghosts peering from behind a curtain?"

"Shhhh. I'm also trying to listen." Sara could block out all superficial sounds and focus her attention on one area. In this case, she was listening for sounds from inside the house. There were creaks and groans, typical house sounds of aging wood. "You did notice the road we turned in from was Fenton Road, the street where Rick Jensen's car was found."

"Yep. All roads lead back to the haunted mansion." They had almost missed the turn since tall hedges appeared to guard the property and a tangle of overgrowth discouraged any curiosity seekers from getting too close. Although the driveway they had traveled was asphalt, grass and weeds had found a way to break through over the years in an attempt to cover its existence. Nature was even attempting to hide the mansion itself as thick ivy had clawed its way up the face of the stone structure.

They climbed back into the Navigator and drove the short distance to the turn around. Dagger parked and they climbed out. A figure on the veranda walked down the stone steps to greet them.

"Sergeant Jackson, Indiana State Police. Chief Wozniak told me you would be coming." Dagger introduced himself and Sara. Jackson had an appreciative smile for Sara. "Need a hand?"

"I can handle it," Dagger snarled.

"Sure," Sara countered with a smile as she opened the trunk of the Navigator. "We have a friend coming shortly who will need a hand with electronic equipment. Are you spending the night?"

Jackson held up his hands. "No thanks. I think I've had my fill of this place. Why do you think I'm staying outside? It's really creepy being in there alone." He grabbed the cooler and headed up the stairs.

Dagger took a few seconds to ponder Simon's warnings. He tried to tell himself he wasn't jealous of anyone who looked at Sara. His problem was that his last injury proved he wasn't invincible. It had taken a toll on him, not so much the threat to his life but where the threat was coming from...BettaTec. This was a threat he felt completely powerless against. His fingers touched the cord necklace. All he had to do was rip it off of his neck and let BettaTec satellites discover him and zap him into oblivion. Then it would be all over. No more waiting and wondering.

"Hey." Sara touched his fingers. Looking into her eyes, seeing the complete confidence she had in the necklace always made him shove those feeling into the deep recesses of his brain. "Come on, lazy. You can only play injured for so long." Her left hand settled on his side where he had been shot. It was more of a caress then a touch. What was it Simon had said?

Just as they started to empty the Navigator, a Humvee rumbled up the drive and parked behind them. The skies overhead were beginning to darken as clouds gathered on the horizon.

"Holy sheeiiit." Skizzy peeled off his mirrored sunglasses and stared up at the massive structure. "Are we gonna have fun tonight." He looked ready for a war in camouflage cargo pants, ribbed undershirt, and a camouflage quilted shirt. Skizzy took a step back when he saw Jackson. "You didn't say there would be cops here."

"I'm not staying," Jackson announced. "As soon as Sergeant Martinez gets here, I'm leaving."

"Padre?" Skizzy's head swiveled toward Dagger. "You didn't say Padre would be here."

"Need someone to arrest the ghosts when they show up." Dagger grabbed one of the metal cases from the back of the Humvee.

"Oh, yeah. That's good." Skizzy pulled an AK-47 from the back. "This here's my ghost buster special."

"Whoa." Jackson made a one-eighty turn. "I didn't just see that."

"Can we hurry up and get inside? I want to tour the house." Sara hefted a grocery bag in her arms, ignoring the weapon in Skizzy's hand.

"Jeez, Skizzy," Dagger whispered. "I don't think a bullet is going to stop a ghost."

"Don't mean the ghost hunters won't pull a fast one. Gotta be prepared."

"Shit." Dagger shook his head and as he passed Jackson said, "Be glad you're leaving."

25 Skizzy chatted incessantly as they crossed the entryway into the foyer. Then everyone stopped. Even Skizzy was stunned into silence. Having seen the house before, Jackson continued into the library. But the rest stood gaping at the sweeping staircase, their heads slowly craning to view the open floor which stretched to the domed ceiling. The scent of aged wood, dust and a moldy odor of a home closed up for too long assaulted them.

"That's one helluva turn-of-the-century skylight." A shiver ran through Skizzy's bony frame.

The staircase was at least fifteen feet wide with a Persian runner covering most of the stairs. Brass light sconces lined the walls while ornate cherry wood cabinets and chairs provided a welcome center.

"It's beautiful," Sara gasped. "The entire house is like something off of a movie set." She turned a slow three-sixty as she studied the thick wood moulding along the walls and the railing on the second floor. "Want to tour the house with us?" Sara asked Skizzy.

"Later. I've got too much to do," Skizzy replied. "Besides, you've seen one haunted house, you've seen them all."

Jackson crossed the floor with a stack of blankets.

"I think that's everything out of the vehicles. All of your equipment is on the conference table and there are outlets in the floor under the table. I would suggest you not use any of the fireplaces. Insurance purposes, according to the attorney." He disappeared into the library and returned several seconds later. "I'll wait for Padre outside. Once he gets here, I'm going to take off. You better set out some backup batteries," Jackson suggested. "I hear you might need them. And there are more candles in the kitchen. Good luck to you. I think you'll need it."

"Wonder what he meant by that?" Skizzy mumbled as they watched Jackson walk out. Another chill shook his body. "Place is like a mausoleum."

Sara agreed and wrapped her leather jacket tighter around her body. "It's a good thing we brought blankets." She led the way to the library.

Two walls were covered with bookcases. Large area rugs dotted the floor, separating clusters of chairs and couches into intimate groupings. Tall windows covered one wall where French doors opened out onto the back patio.

Skizzy said, "Room looks like the lobby at the Hilton Hotel."

"When were you at the Hilton?" Dagger hoped Skizzy wasn't going to cop to bugging the hotel.

"I get around."

Sara pulled on Dagger's sleeve. "Come on. Let's check the place out before Padre and the rest get here."

They started on the first floor, making their way down a lengthy hallway. Even years of dust hadn't dulled the wood floors or chair rails. There was marble in the foyer and entryway, even some on the tabletops. Cobwebs and dead insect carcasses crowding in corners were the only things that marred the elegance. They stepped into an open room sectioned off from the hallway by marble pillars. There was a brass plate on one of the pillars which said, *The Gathering*.

Sara ran a hand over the plate. "The Historical Society must have added the signs when the house was open for tours."

"Fancy name for a living room."

"Look at this place, Dagger." Sara crossed the room, stepping on thick Persian rugs and dodging upholstered chairs. A marble counter in a semi-circle was in one corner of the room. "Must have been a bar. There's a sink and an opening for a small refrigerator."

A wall of windows looked out onto what might have once been a garden. Dagger waved a hand in front of the glass. "Place is pretty well built. Can't even feel a draft." The yard outside the windows was overgrown with brush and dead stalks. A fountain filled with stagnant water listed at the center of a crowd of bushes long past a trim.

They made their way further down the hall to a more intimate enclosure. The sign outside the entrance said *Tranquility*. There were window seats lining a bay window. An octagon-shaped table was near one wall by a fireplace.

"Another fancy name for what? A *leave me in peace* room?" Dagger walked over and started pressing on the paneled wall.

"Think there's some secret opening?"

"One never knows." Dagger checked the inside of the fireplace, pushing on the back bricks. He brushed the soot from his hands and looked up at the ceiling. It was at least twenty feet high without a trap door in sight. He shoved the sleeves up on his gray sweater. The collar of a black and gray shirt peeked out from the sweater's crew neck.

"Come on. Let's check out the second floor before it gets too dark. It's supposed to have twelve bedrooms, six bathrooms, a nursery, study."

They made their way back to the foyer and climbed the sweeping staircase. "Would you like to live in a house this big?" Dagger asked.

"No way. It's too big. But it's history. That's the appeal. This was the first house to have all the modern conveniences years before a normal John Q. Public could afford them. According to Padre this ghost hunter group is supposed to have all the background on everyone who had lived here over the years. That should make for some interesting reading."

"Provided they didn't make it all up."

Sara sighed deeply. "Have you always been this cynical?"

"Everyone has an angle. Just remember that, Sara."

"Wow." Stretched in front of them was a long corridor which ended in a wall of windows. To the left and right of them were hallways leading to rooms. Skizzy was right. The place did look like a five star hotel. Sara rushed to the end of the corridor. The curved windows gave a view of what might have been a lush green yard and manicured hedges in its day. To the right was the view of a large terrace off of one of the rooms. An identical terrace was off one of the rooms on her left.

"I want to see the terrace." Sara ran back toward the staircase and down one of the hallways to the first room. All of the doors on the second floor were open. She hurried through a room wallpapered in a rose design which matched the upholstered chairs. It appeared to be a sitting room of some type, maybe a study. She turned the door knobs on the French doors and stepped out onto the terrace.

Dirt, leaves, and branches littered the tiled floor. If there had been any tables or chairs at one time, they had been removed. Sara walked to the edge of the terrace and looked over the concrete railing.

Dagger slowly made his way next to her and leaned his arms on the barrier. "I don't know. The Tyler mansion puts this one to shame."

"The Tyler mansion is just newer and cleaner. If anyone ever put any time or money into this place, I think it would really be something."

Dagger turned and looked up at the turrets. "Damn, those gargoyles are ugly."

Sara followed his gaze but her eyes drifted to one of the dormer windows near the roof. A shiver ran through her body.

"Are you cold?" Dagger wrapped an arm around her shoulder and pulled her close. The overcast skies had dropped the temperatures at least fifteen degrees. "Come on. Let's see if we can find the big bad ghost."

They made sure the French doors were locked before returning to the hallway. Wall sconces along the way clicked on, illuminating the hallway. The bedrooms were cookie-cutter replicas from window treatments and Persian rugs to the canopy beds and dressing tables. It was as though the owner had received a quantity discount on the mansion's furnishings. At the end of the hall they saw a brass plate—*Curriculum.*

"I wonder if the children were home schooled," Sara asked. The room contained recessed book cases, work stations, an easel, and one massive desk set in a corner. The floor was hardwood without a rug to protect its finish. "The Historical Society supposedly made sure to replace any damaged furnishings with replicas. If this room didn't have carpeting then they didn't add one."

"Or someone used it to roll up a body."

They returned the way they had come and stopped at what looked like a child's room. The canopy bed and dust ruffle were in pink and white eyelet. The dressing table had a matching skirt and upholstered lid on the bench seat. A music box sat in the middle of the dresser top. Sara ran a hand along the top. "Not one speck of dust. How can that be?" She lifted the lid on the music box. It played what sounded like a Viennese waltz. "Pretty." Sara closed the box then walked over to the bed. Lying against the pillows was a doll dressed in the same color eyelet as the bedspread. One eye was closed, its lashes touching a chubby cheek. Suddenly the closed eye popped open. Sara jumped back.

"Bet the damn head turns, too," Dagger said. "And what the hell happened to its hair?"

"The girl probably combed it too hard. Hair wasn't as tightly woven back then."

They continued down the hall on the opposite side of the staircase, taking a passing glance in each of the doorways. "Padre checked the blueprints on this house?" Sara asked.

"He and Leyton Monroe both. Forensics went through the house room by room. No panic rooms, attics or locked pantries."

"What about fireplaces that moved?" Sara nodded toward a fireplace in what looked like the master suite.

"All of the fireplaces are on an outer wall. No place for them to move to."

"Maybe down. Did they check the ones on the first floor?"

"There's a root cellar under the kitchen and dining room but they checked it out. Didn't find any kind of an entrance to the floor above except through the trap door on the outside of the house." He studied his partner, the intensity in her eyes, how they changed to an elliptical shape when she called on the eyesight of the hawk. "Do you hear or sense anything out of the ordinary?"

Sara shook her head. "I've been listening for labored breathing, cries, slow heartbeat of someone unconscious, even a fast heartbeat of someone injured. I don't sense anything, Dagger. I already checked the exterior. Where do you think Sheila could be?"

"My money's still on Paris."

26 Padre lead the way into the mansion. Josh, dressed in baggy shorts and a tee shirt, grumbled like an impudent child. "Don't know why we couldn't bring our own equipment."

"Our department is checking it out," Padre replied. "You'll get it all back."

They entered the foyer and Flea came to an abrupt stop. Dagger stood at the bottom of the staircase, arms crossed. Exposed in a holster on the right side of his waist was a Kimber .45. Eyes oozed distrust and fingers twitched as though ready for any false move from the visitors.

"Whoa. Who's the scary dude? *Witchblade.* Remember that show, Josh?"

Josh felt Dagger's glare. The eyes were so black Josh was sure if he looked close he would probably see his own reflection in them. "Damn, yeah," he whispered. "What was that character's name?"

Flea snapped his fingers several times. "Nottingham. Ian Nottingham. Show ran for two seasons. Could never figure out if the character was a good guy or a bad guy."

Venus pulled up close to Flea and studied the stranger. "Yeah, totally scary...umm, but sexy."

Padre worked his way around the three. "Josh, Curt, Venus, meet Chase Dagger. Dagger is a consultant for the police department." Not one member reached out to shake his hand. Josh and Flea gave a limp wave while Venus studied him as though he were some specimen.

"How strange," Venus said. "Your aura is like totally black."

Skizzy and Sara emerged from the library. Skizzy scrutinized the group in much the same way Dagger had. Flea could be Skizzy in thirty years. But the two young men had their attention elsewhere. Like frozen beams of light, Sara's turquoise eyes had them mesmerized. Their eyes roamed from the navy blue corduroys that hugged her legs to the cowl neck sweater that hit mid-thigh. Her boots were dark blue suede and reached just above the ankles. Their attempt to speak left their mouths in silent perpetual motion, like fish gasping for breath.

Venus stepped forward. "I hope I don't slip on their drool." She reached a hand out to Sara. "Don't mind them. They don't get out much. I'm Venus."

Padre finished the introductions. "Sara, Skizzy, meet Curt, and Josh."

"Flea," Curt said, clearing his throat. "You can call me Flea."

"Damn, you smell good," Josh said in a halting voice. He saw Dagger roll his eyes. "Uh, what is it you do?"

Skizzy jerked his head toward Dagger. "She keeps him from shooting people."

"Skizzy is our electronics expert." Padre waved his arm toward the room. "Shall we move this little meet and greet to the library?"

"What kinda name is Flea?" Skizzy asked.

"What kinda name is Skizzy?" Flea's gaze drifted to the equipment on the conference table. "Wow. All this stuff yours?"

"Wonderful," Dagger deadpanned. "They are bonding over electronics."

"Now they'll be engaged in geek-speak for the rest of the night," Josh said.

Padre gave a high-sign at Dagger saying, "Let's take a walk." He led Dagger through the foyer and back out onto the veranda. "Thought you should see where the bodies were found." Padre had stopped at home to change out of his professional clothes. Now he looked as though he were going camping in his blue jeans, a turtleneck, flannel shirt, and loafers.

They walked through trampled grass around toward the back of the house. It was easy to see how a house this size had been hidden for so long. It was surrounded on three sides by woods and enough hedges had been planted on the street side that, when fully grown, they had tightly woven together to form a green wall.

"How much property did Sebold own?" Dagger asked.

"About seventy-five acres. No one can build around him because it's all forest preserve property."

"Anyone check to see if there were hunting blinds in the forest?" Dagger dodged a patch of mud, thankful that he had worn boots instead of tennis shoes.

"Sergeant Jackson contacted the ranger station. They don't allow the building of any hunting structures in the forest."

They reached an area where crime scene tape floated in the afternoon breeze. It surrounded a ditch filled with dried leaves and a five-inch deep accumulation of water from the recent storm.

"This is where Rick Jensen was found." Padre turned toward the house. "As you can see, it isn't exactly a straight line from the back door. Where he came from is anyone's guess. He might as well have fallen out of the sky."

"There has got to be some kind of cellar in that house that has remained undetected. What else can explain it?" Dagger studied the low hanging clouds as though Padre's comment held any credence. "What's the weather prediction?"

"Massive storm front heading our way. Exactly where I want to be during a killer storm...a haunted house."

Dagger had to chuckle at that. "Maybe we'll need you to do an exorcism."

"Don't joke about it. Come on. Let me show you the well." Padre led the way down a trampled path. They could see the tire tracks from the vehicles that had driven through yesterday. Some tall grass stood as thick as a corn field. Others had fallen in layers, struck down by the guardsmen. "How have you been feeling?"

"Been talking to Sara?"

"Yeah, right. She's about as forthcoming as you are. You look the same, although I'm glad you got rid of the beard. I was ready to put your name on the terrorist watch list."

"Sara's tough to argue with when she has a straight edge in her hand."

Padre stopped and pointed at a slab of concrete. "This is the entrance to the well. Took four guys to remove it. They had to pretty much use a machete on all the overgrowth so it was obvious no one had been around in years."

Dagger did a slow scan of the acres surrounding the house. It was as well protected as the three hundred acres Sara's house sat on. "I don't know, Padre. If she were here, we would have found her by now. Sara and I did a walk through most of the first floor but only a quick look through the rooms upstairs. I didn't find a dummy waiter or attic entrance much less boarded over closets. Skizzy brought some type of scanner that sees through walls. Your guys didn't find a storm shelter or second root cellar?"

"No, and before you ask, we checked the airline passenger lists. She's not on any of them, hasn't used her passport."

"She's pretty persuasive with her assistants by threat of firing. I wouldn't put it past Sheila to have her assistant drive over, pick her up, and drive her to a private jet at a small airport."

"Already checked the assistant."

"And you don't think she'd lie to protect her job?"

"Leyton Monroe can also be pretty persuasive."

The kitchen was industrial-sized with a center work station and cabinets on three of the walls. Sara opened a large cooler and pulled out two of the foot-long sandwiches.

"You should see the butler's pantry. It's bigger than

my kitchen at home." Venus dug through the bags and pulled out paper plates and napkins. "The counter should be clean. I wiped it down the day we arrived," Venus said. "So you work with, what was his name?"

"Dagger. Padre sometimes calls us in to consult on cases, especially the unusual ones. And this one is definitely unusual."

"Do you carry a gun?"

"Not today. Dagger usually carries an arsenal." Sara didn't think she would need a gun this weekend. She hadn't even brought a purse. She studied Venus's long dress, tattoos, and colorful jewelry and remembered what Padre had said about her. Venus would fit right in behind a crystal ball at a carnival. "Have you always been interested in astrology and the occult?"

"It started in high school. That's when most of my friends started carving out their own passions. There were three of us who got into Wiccan. We would do chants in the forest, dress in all black, claim to put spells on the guys we liked."

Sara could almost picture Venus in a forest dancing around a circle drawn in the dirt, candles balancing in the center. "Any of it work?"

"No. We were all fans of the TV show *Charmed* and thought it would be fun." Venus placed cans of soda on the table. They found packets of mayonnaise and mustard in the Subway bag.

"How do you like investigating haunted houses?" It had been Dagger's suggestion that they each engage the IPI members in casual conversation hoping one would slip up and reveal more of what happened the night Sheila disappeared.

"My grandmother and mother both believed they were witches. Claimed to have out-of-body experiences while they slept. I guess you could say it was kind of bred in me, although I was too young to understand until I was in my teens. There is a lot of energy in the world, things we can't see. Who's to say what's real and what isn't? My grandmother taught me how to do seances and communicate with the departed souls who were looking for answers, trying to find their way to the light."

"I'm sure that concept is difficult for some people to accept. Was Sheila open-minded about it?"

Venus laughed. Sara detected a flash of loathing in Venus's eyes. But Venus reined it in as she replied, "I could tell the moment I saw her that it was all a joke to her. She posed for the photos, tried to hide her skepticism but it was thinly veiled." Venus lifted the strands of colorful beads on her neck. "She even fingered these as though they were the tackiest things she had ever seen. I just knew she wasn't doing an unbiased reporting of our work. I honestly believe she planned to do a scathing article."

"Is that how Josh and Flea felt?"

"Oh, puleeze. It's a wonder they didn't trip over their tongues watching her strut around here. She has an air about her, that subtle body language that says to keep your distance, yet she flirts, wanting, I guess, to make sure she has the attention of every man in the room. She had them wrapped around her little finger. Men are so transparent."

Sara thought this was as good a time to try to bond

with her new friend. "Sheila used to be engaged to Dagger."

Venus almost dropped a can of soda. "You have got to be kidding. Her auras and his are so not compatible. How did that ever happen?"

Sara realized Venus referred to Sheila in the present term, not past, as someone might do if they knew Sheila were dead. "She's a bit controlling and Dagger doesn't like to be controlled."

Venus lifted the cooler and placed it on the counter. She moved the cans of soda around so the ice could keep them cold. "Did you know Dagger then?"

"That's when I first met him. I asked for his help on another case. It was a couple days before his wedding rehearsal. The case made him so late he didn't bother going."

"The case." Venus smiled. Iridescent glitter flaked off of her eye shadow and landed on her cheeks. "You are clueless about your appeal to men, especially Dagger. You should have seen his reaction when Josh and Flea almost tripped over their tongues looking at you. I can imagine Sheila saw the same effect you had on Dagger."

"Dagger has always had a big brother complex. It's been all business between us. If Sheila read more into it, that was her problem." Sara tried to steer the focus back to Venus. "What about Josh and Flea? Are you dating either of them?"

"Oh, no. I have a girlfriend."

"Oh." That revelation surprised Sara but she tried not to let it show. "Well, then, how did you feel about Sheila?"

Venus laughed. "She's definitely too rich and elitist

for my blood. Astrid and I have been together since high school."

"Is Astrid into astrology, too?"

"Believe it or not, she's a molecular physicist."

"That should make for interesting dinner conversation."

"Thank you."

"For what?"

"Most people just can't see what a brain like Astrid would see in someone like me. Truth is, I have a Mensa I.Q. and a degree in botany. But it fed my interest in herbs and Nature's marvelous healing plants. Astrid was part of my Wiccan group in high school so she understands my interest in astrology and tarot cards and everything that is unexplainable."

"Like ghosts and spirits."

"Exactly."

Padre stuck his head in the doorway. "Girls need a hand? We're about ready to chew on the woodwork out here."

27

After grabbing plates and cans of pop from the kitchen, everyone gathered around the conference table. Skizzy's laptop was set up at one end of the table. Two file folders on the table contained research notes which the IPI group had left from their first night there. Venus brought the bags of potato chips and cheese curls from the kitchen and placed them on the table.

"Don't you have any EMF meters or any other equipment, dude?" Flea asked. "No cameras or recorders?"

"Got all kinds of special goodies." Skizzy held up what looked like a geiger counter. "This here reads natural electro-magnetic impulses. Also have a scanner that sees through walls. Whether the victim is dead or alive, I'll know it." His one eyebrow jerked as if to add, "So beware."

Josh glared across the table at Padre. "Now that we are all gathered for our Thanksgiving dinner, tell us exactly why we are here, and the truth this time. Not some bullshit about needing to see for your own eyes exactly what happens in a haunted house. Why the private investigator?" He glared at Dagger with suspicion.

Skizzy pulled out a chair and sprawled into it. "Why, don't you see? We are here to investigate you three."

Padre jumped in before Josh could voice his objection. "Leyton Monroe hired Dagger and his team to figure out what happened to his daughter. I'm here because I still haven't cleared the three of you. You were the last three to see her. Something happened in this house and it's up to me, with Dagger's help, to figure out what."

"And what if we don't want to stay?" Flea asked.

"You either stay here with me or I put you in a cell until I figure it out on my own. Your choice. Besides," he reached in his pocket and held up a set of keys, "I'm driving."

Flea studied his sandwich, then reluctantly took a bite.

Sara remained silent, preferring to listen to what was not being said as much as what was being said. Josh was combative while Flea was suspicious. Venus appeared calm as if she had just finished a thirty minute yoga class. It probably wasn't the first time she had to be the only sane member of her group.

Josh waved his half-eaten sandwich at the end of the table. "What else aren't you telling us? What's with all this equipment and this lone gunman look-alike," he added with a poke toward Skizzy, whose ponytail and camouflage pants did make him resemble a character from the TV show, *X-Files*. "A private eye is one thing, but why do we need another computer geek? It's just a duplicate of what Flea's doing."

Padre stared across the table at Dagger. An unspoken agreement appeared to pass between them. Padre patted his mouth with a napkin and cleared his throat. "There is another detail that we have kept out of the paper."

Their three guests appeared to hold a collective

breath. Dagger watched them closely. Skizzy poured more chips onto his paper plate while Padre explained about the two bodies found in a dried well.

Venus gasped. "Two more?" She slapped a hand against her throat, the circle of bracelets clanging on her wrist. "Who? Where?"

A slow drizzle started pelting the wall of windows. Outside thick clouds crawled, dragging a dark sky behind like a cape, as though needing to hide any destruction it planned.

"The well is about one hundred feet from the house. Searchers were chopping their way through the underbrush but it's the cadaver dogs that found the well. It had a concrete cover over the opening. They had to pry it up and it was evident it hadn't been accessed in decades."

"So they may be the people haunting the house. Have they identified them? Do you know when they died?" Venus's questions were coming fast and furious.

"No and maybe," Padre replied. "But that's not the important thing. The bodies are one male and one female. They were dressed in period clothes, possibly from the early 1900s. But the puzzling, possibly shocking detail is that they were killed the same way as the man we found in the ditch."

"What do you mean the same way?" Josh asked.

"Strangled, but this time with rope. The ropes were tied in the identical way the scarf was tied around Mister Jensen's neck. And although it isn't tough for anyone, even me, to tie a bow, it is just too much of a coincidence to find victims, at least eighty years apart, to have died the same way. And I don't like coincidences."

"Wow, noxious." Flea's eyes widened making them appear even larger behind his thick glasses. "We have a real paranormal event happening here."

"How can that be? I mean..." Josh leaned back against his seat.

Dagger thought he looked like the boy who cried wolf only to face a real wolf. He always thought there was something deceptive about what Josh and his ilk do. He had yet to see proof that ghosts were trying to communicate or that the dead were in some limbo with unresolved issues. Then again, two years ago he would have never admitted shapeshifters were real or there was technology that could make people invisible. His cases lately have been anything but logical.

"What does Sara bring to the table?" Josh asked. "Or..." His index finger waved from Dagger to Sara. "Are you two...?"

Dagger and Sara replied too quickly, "NO," while Skizzy, at the same time blurted, "Not yet."

Dagger ignored the insinuation. "Sara has talents that are important to my investigations."

"I bet she does," Josh said under his breath.

"Tell us about the house," Sara said in an attempt to change the subject.

Outside the wind tore leaves from the weeping willows, sending them skittering across the landscape. There was a faint rumble in the distance, but if the wind kept up its strength, it wouldn't be long until the storm hit them full force.

Josh took the lead and appeared to have researched the house thoroughly because he didn't refer to any notes. "It was built in the early 1940s by Charles Sebold. Chucky was a shipping tycoon who developed the lake front harbor. He and his wife, Marian, had one child, a daughter named Julia. This little brick bungalow has twelve bedrooms, five bathrooms, a ballroom, huge industrial-sized kitchen for entertaining the rich and famous, a library, kids playroom, massive gardens, servants quarters, you name it. The rich spared no expense."

"So whose ghost were you hoping to rattle?" Padre asked.

"Julia is the one whose presence is still in this house," Venus interjected. "She is the one I was trying to contact."

"She went missing when she was seven," Josh continued. "The staff lived on site and all were cleared of any involvement. After a year without any clues, Marian was so despondent she committed suicide."

"In this house?" Padre asked.

"No. Witnesses say she walked off one of the piers in the harbor. Chucky informed all of his business partners that he was moving to Texas after her funeral. Instead, he took a header off of the upstairs veranda."

"Huh," Skizzy blurted. "How do you know it isn't the wife who's haunting the place?"

"Because there have only been reports of sounds from Julia's room," Josh replied.

Dagger continued eating while Josh spoke. He noticed Sara was staring at her hands as though not listening, but Dagger knew there was more to it. He knew

Sara was listening to the beating of Josh's heart. She may as well be a human lie detector test. It surprised him that she was able to focus only on Josh and block out everyone else's breathing and heartbeats.

"Who bought the house after that?" Padre asked.

"Sat empty for ten years, not that there weren't plenty of lookers. Few people could afford it. Then a Chicago businessman bought it. Brent Boseman traveled a lot, leaving his young bride alone with a staff of five. A staff member was found dead one morning at the bottom of the staircase. It was ruled an accident. Other staff members claimed they had heard him cry out, heard him yell 'no,' but all the other staff were accounted for. Then one by one the staff quit, claiming they were hearing cries in the middle of the night, footsteps. The wife refused to stay in the house one more night so the house was empty again for another fifteen years."

"But Mister Boseman did bring in a priest to do an exorcism at the request of his wife," Venus explained. "He wasn't too happy to move so he agreed to his wife's request. When that didn't work, she wanted a medium to contact whoever was haunting the place. The medium claimed there was a lot of evil in the house. That did it for the wife."

"Well, I hope my presence doesn't piss off the ghost," Padre muttered under his breath while his fingers found the gold cross he had pulled from under his shirt.

"After that a curator rented it to set up a museum but too many weird sounds, footsteps, lights flickering. Workers claimed they always felt as though someone were watching them. Then the Historical Society gave it a go but the upkeep was too expensive and there weren't enough donations coming in. They claimed the house was cursed."

"Mass hysteria," Dagger chimed in. "Not unusual. They hear stories or read about the history of the place and soon everyone is seeing ghosts."

"Government research plan," Skizzy quipped. "I've seen it before. Government puts people in a situation to see how they react, see what it takes to drive someone to suicide or drive them to the looney bin."

Josh sneered at him. "That what happened to you?"

Skizzy's eyebrow jutted sharply as he glared at Josh. "I wouldn't be so quick to dismiss it, boy. I've seen more in my lifetime than anything your fancy equipment would ever pick up."

"Let's keep on subject," Padre quickly interjected.

Dagger asked, "How did you get the current owner to agree to let you set up shop here?"

"We had to clear it with some lawyer first. He thought the publicity would draw prospective buyers," Venus replied. "With the popularity of all the ghost hunting shows, they thought it would draw people the way some of the allegedly haunted restaurants and hotels draw record number patrons."

"So you were going to film what happened here and hope to sell it to a cable network to do what? Get your own show?" Dagger didn't care if his comment sounded cynical.

"Hell, yeah," Flea said with a laugh. "Who wouldn't?"

Josh studied the equipment and computer Skizzy had

set up. "Wait a minute." He narrowed his eyes at Skizzy. "Are you here to make your own movie and compete with us? Because if you are..."

"Do I look like a freakin' movie producer?" Actually, Skizzy looked more like a mad scientist, but then some movie producers did display a bit of creative madness.

"Tell us about your most exciting trip," Sara said. "Did you ever catch one on film? Did one ever touch you?"

"Did anyone ever die before?" Dagger's gaze settled on Josh.

"What is this? An inquisition? Are we being set up?" Josh looked at Padre. "Well?"

"Do you feel like you are being set up?"

"You are asking a lot of questions, dude," Flea said.

"Got a problem with that?" Dagger drilled him with his eyes. "I'm about to spend the night with three people I don't know a damn thing about."

"Yeah, he does have a trigger finger," Skizzy added.

"Not very trusting, are you?" Josh sneered. "We could say the same thing. We don't know a damn thing about you three."

"There are few people I trust and for good reason."

"I want to hear more about the history." Sara started to gather up the empty plates while Venus retrieved a large plastic garbage bag. "Were there any other theories about the deaths?"

"The Rain Man," Venus replied. "There was a book written by Theodore Lautenburg. He documented a number of murders from 1920 to 1950. They took place mainly in this area and over the borders of Illinois and

Michigan. That is where the comparison to the Boston Strangler came in. The killer would strangle his victims with a scarf."

"Tied in a bow?" Padre didn't recall any previous cases in the computer but then they all took place over fifty years ago. "Why call the killer Rain Man?"

"Because, he only killed during a storm." A clap of thunder almost drowned out Venus's words. "He killed fourteen people. There would be a storm followed by a rash of killings, then nothing for another ten years."

"Sounds like folklore to me." Dagger tossed his empty plate in the garbage. "I would sooner concentrate on the here and now."

"I agree," Padre said. "We need to look for a missing woman."

"I want to finish looking through the rooms," Dagger said. "Maybe there's something your men missed."

"We'll help," Josh offered.

"No." The last thing Dagger wanted were two love sick puppies following them around. He picked up one of the scanners Skizzy brought. "Why don't you take your scanner and finish the first floor, Skizzy."

"Yo, dude. That the gadget you were talking about?" Flea rose from the table and walked over to where Skizzy stood.

"Yep, dude." Skizzy stressed the word Flea had a tendency to overuse. "Why don't you tag along?" Skizzy checked the battery in the scanner.

"So anything you might have hidden in a wall will now be found." Dagger sensed something not quite right with the IPI group, or at least the two guys. Was he only getting territorial and over-protective of Sara?

"Are you accusing us of something?" Josh demanded. "Just because you swagger in here with a gun on your hip gives you no right..."

"ENOUGH!" Padre's head was ready to split and his frustration was bested by a grumbling of thunder. "Give me the second scanner. Josh and I will start at the other end of the house."

"Do you hear it?" Venus pointed toward the window. "It's starting to really come down. I better light the candles." She grabbed the box of matches off the mantle.

"Let it storm," Skizzy said, rubbing his hands together. "We have our snacks, candles, and Padre has his crucifix. We're good to go." He grabbed the scanner and set off.

Lightning flashed beyond the windows and several seconds later a large crash of thunder shook the building. The lights began to flicker.

At the top of the staircase against the darkness of the alcove, an image attempted to cut through a haze. It hovered, changing shape, pressing against some unseen veil as it gathered strength to fully materialize. Outside, as the storm intensified, the figure frantically ripped through the veil, took in the sounds from the floor below, then stepped back and waited.

28 "That is a beautiful doll." Sheila wasn't too surprised that the doll was dressed in the same type of Victorian clothes as Colleen wore. "I used to have a bed full of dolls. I swear, every time a new Barbie doll came out, I had to have it."

"What's a Barbeeee," Colleen asked, dragging the name out as though it had three syllables.

"Oh, come on. You had to have heard of Barbie and Ken." Sheila studied the intricate lace work on the doll's clothing. Colleen shook her head no. Of course not, Sheila thought. In her dream she had been dropped into another era, like Dorothy in *The Wizard of Oz*. You would think she could at least feel her mother holding her hand. She wondered briefly if Dagger might be there, too. Unless her father was there in which case Dagger wouldn't be anywhere near. Would be nice to open her eyes and find Joe and Dagger on opposite sides of her bed, each holding her hand, promising undying love. She gazed quickly at Walker and thought of how often she had had sex in her dreams. At least being in a coma wouldn't be a total loss. He did have a dangerous appeal, sinister and dark, like Dagger. Joe had a bit of bad boy in him, but not the dangerous undercurrent Dagger possessed. Whereas Dagger's danger left a thrill coursing through her body,

Walker's was more Dexter-like. Some men undress Sheila with their eyes. With Walker he appeared more to be gutting her.

"What are those?" Colleen pointed at the colorful bands around Sheila's wrist.

"They are animal bands." Sheila peeled them off and placed them on her lap. "See how this one is shaped like a dog? The blue one is a bird. And this one is a squirrel. Here." Sheila slipped them on Colleen's wrist. "I gave a tour of our newspaper headquarters to a group of grade schoolers several weeks ago. Each of the students gave me one of their bands."

"What are you supposed to do with them?"

"The kids exchange them, like baseball cards."

"I remember those," Walker said as he had been quietly listening to their conversation. "I've shown them to you, Colleen."

But Colleen either didn't remember or had no interest. She was more focused on the rubber bands. She carefully counted the bands, placing them in two piles, careful to make sure they were even.

"Are they mine to keep?" Colleen's eyes were wide in anticipation. It looked as though Colleen had never received a gift before. Was the one doll Colleen played with the only toy this child owned?

"Tell you what. Why don't you take ten and I'll take ten. That will make us like a big sister/little sister."

Colleen agreed and handed one stack to Sheila.

A bolt of lightning lit up the skies followed by a clap of thunder they could feel through the floor boards. Colleen stiffened and even Sheila felt her body jerk. Walker only smiled and looked longingly at the skies.

Sheila picked up the doll and straightened its dress. "I saw one similar to this one somewhere. It had been propped against the pillows on a pink bedspread." Sheila thought about that for several seconds. "Of course! This is wonderful!"

"And how does this make you deliriously happy?" Adrian prompted. He sat with his back against the couch's arm rest, his body cocked to face her. Colleen sat on the floor cross-legged, her eyes riveted from Adrian to Sheila.

"Because now that more of my memory is returning, it means I'm coming out of the coma. Don't you see?" Adrian and Colleen exchanged glances. Sheila prattled on but neither of them appeared willing to challenge her.

"Sebold founded the shipping harbor which brought a lot of business to the area. He built the mansion on the outskirts of what is now Cedar Point. After he and his family left...no." Sheila closed her eyes for a few seconds. "No, something happened to his daughter and wife. But why was I in his house?" She rubbed the bump on the back of her head. It was still tender as was the bump on her forehead. "YES!" Sheila cried out as more of her memory came back. "That's where I was. I joined this group of amateur ghost hunters when they spent the night at the mansion."

Colleen giggled. Adrian smiled. "Ghosts? How amusing."

"Do you believe in ghosts?" Colleen asked her.

"Not at all. And you shouldn't either." Sheila

touched Colleen's cheek. "There is a logical explanation for everything...like my coma."

"What happened to her?" Colleen's voice was so low Sheila wasn't sure she heard her correctly.

"Who, sweetie?"

"The man's daughter? You said something happened to her."

Sheila struggled to remember the names. "Marian was the wife and...Julia. Yes, Charles and Marian Sebold had a daughter Julia. She disappeared when she was seven years old. Never seen again."

"What do they think happened to her?"

Adrian slowly straightened, his dark gaze leveled on Colleen. "Miss Monroe, I don't believe this is a subject for someone Colleen's age."

"I'm seven, too." Colleen appeared eager to find out more about Julia Sebold. "Did her daddy miss her?"

"I'm sure he did."

"Miss Monroe." Adrian's voice was abrupt. Outside a line of dark clouds charged angrily across the skies. Colleen inched closer to Sheila. She studied her hands, averting her eyes from Adrian.

29 "How strange. Why do we still have lights downstairs but not upstairs?" Sara moved slowly to keep the candle from being extinguished.

Dagger slapped his flashlight against his leg. "Damn thing worked downstairs."

"This is the last room. Padre said Sheila had claimed this room for herself. Her purse and coat were found here."

How like Sheila to claim the master suite for herself. A large four-poster platform bed was against one wall. Candlelight caused shadows to dip and sway around desks and chairs, playing a surreal game of hide and seek. Sara lifted the candle toward the wall where a painting hung.

"This must be Marian and Julia. How beautiful." The two were mirror reflections of each other. Both had blonde hair and blue eyes. Marian had a hint of haughtiness but the smile on her face and softness of her features played it down. Julia looked around five years of age. They were sitting on a bench in the gardens. The colors in the portrait were bright, the day sunny. Sara noticed the artist's signature. "Her husband painted this."

Dagger closed the closet door. "There's nothing here. Not even an access to a hidden passageway."

A movement outside the door caught Sara's attention.

It was a quick flash as though the darkness shifted. "Hold this." Sara handed Dagger the candleholder and stepped out of the room. She called on the eyesight of the hawk and surveyed the hall to her left. She didn't see anything or anyone suspicious. Slowly she moved past the staircase and down the opposite hall. A crash of thunder brought with it a strobe light of lightning. She cocked her head and heard someone swearing downstairs. The storm probably zapped the power in the entire house. She blocked out the voices but it was difficult to block out the storm. Rain pelted the roof high above her head. She stood in the doorway of the study. Outside the French doors rain gathered in puddles on the terrace. But when the lightning flashed, she suddenly saw a dark figure standing in front of the French doors. What sounded like a whisper drew her attention. Sara's curiosity outweighed her fears. They still didn't have any proof of ghosts or spirits, friendly or evil. But she was sure her enhanced powers could certainly sense any uninvited guests.

The storm had developed an attitude, alternating thunder and lightning in a continuous raucous rhythm. Whatever was standing in front of the French doors was no longer there. Sara was confident the shadow was her imagination. She turned to go back the way she came and was brought face-to-face with what looked like a man. She could see him yet she could see the hallway behind him. He was dressed in a pleated shirt, light color, and he had a scar above his right eye. Through the image she could see Dagger exiting one of the bedrooms at the far end of the hall. For some reason Sara wasn't afraid. She stood her ground and the figure advanced.

Stop him.

What? Stop who? Sara wondered. Did she actually hear words or was the storm playing tricks on her hearing.

The image swayed at first as it advanced closer. For a moment he seemed to disappear but then she felt a breeze on her face, a breath next to her ear.

Stop him.

As Dagger approached, the figure retreated and disappeared, as though stepping behind a curtain.

"Hey, where did you go?" Dagger cupped a hand around the candle flame to keep it from dying out. "Find anything?"

"Do you see anyone near me?"

Dagger looked at her and slowly smiled. "You're not going to tell me you saw a ghost, are you?"

Sara said nothing. She grabbed the candleholder from his grasp and turned, shining the light behind her but it barely reached past ten yards. The storm continued its own light display but the hallway was empty as well as the study.

"He told me to stop him. What do you think that meant?"

Dagger cocked his head and was ready to laugh but Sara wasn't smiling. "You're serious."

"It was Sebold, Dagger. I'm sure of it. He had the scar above his eye, the same one that shows on the portrait downstairs." She stood in the doorway to the study, the room with the terrace where Sebold had jumped to his death. "What if his death wasn't an accident?"

"Come on." Dagger wrapped an arm around her shoulder and led her toward the staircase. "I think you have been listening to too many stories about the Rain Man."

Padre swept the scanner over the wall in the servants' quarters. "Our fire department has a couple of these. Amazing little gadgets." A five-inch monitor jutted from the hand held device. What was on the screen resembled an x-ray image. A gray and white hazy reflection of wiring, beams, and dead space.

"You should have done this yesterday. Would have saved us all a lot of time. I could be back home already." Josh stifled a yawn, not exactly the sign of a guilty man.

"If I could have gotten the fire department out here, I would have. But at the time there wasn't a reason to check the walls. Now open that closet door."

Josh trudged over and pulled the door open. Padre looked for any signs of hesitation from the lanky guy, but he wasn't even breaking a sweat. Padre swept the scanner over the ceiling. Still nothing.

"Sheila Monroe is a beautiful woman. Was she your type?"

Josh let out a snort. "A little too rich and too old for my blood."

"Really? You're only a few years younger. Did she shut you down?"

Josh closed the closet door and followed Padre out of the room. "I know what you're trying to do, Sergeant."

"And what's that?" Padre smiled. He didn't need a

physical interrogation room to break down a suspect. "Two self-made men like you and Flea might think it would be appealing to someone like Miss Monroe. Here she pulls up in that fancy car of hers. She's an heiress to a dynasty of sorts."

"And she was completely out of our league." Having finished their section of the first floor, Josh turned and lumbered back to the library.

The only part of Josh's comment that clung to Padre's ears was how Josh referred to Sheila in the past tense.

30 The library was littered with candles. Outside the skies were hurling sheets of horizontal rain. The loss of electricity didn't bother Dagger. He and Skizzy had brought night vision goggles. Sara had her own version of night vision goggles. He glanced quickly at her. She had been quiet since revealing her alleged encounter with Sebold.

"This is like watching paint dry." Padre flipped open a card in his game of solitaire. "Cell phones don't work, power is out. What a night to be sitting in a haunted house."

"When a spirit is trying to manifest itself," Venus explained, "it draws its energy from whatever source it can."

Sara walked up to Skizzy. "How come your computers still have power?"

"Super duper battery backup."

"Did your scanner detect anything on the first floor?"

"Nope. Walls contain nothing but the typical wiring and pipes." Skizzy pounded away on his laptop.

Flea and Josh sat at the end of the conference table, heads together.

Sara moved to the French doors and watched the storm. It always amazed her the power Nature could release. Although her eyes focused on what was outside the house, her attention was actually focused elsewhere.

"You okay?" Dagger followed her gaze. "I didn't mean to make fun of you."

"Shhhh." She pulled on his sweater to move him closer, then brought her lips close to his ear. "Flea and Josh are talking," Sara whispered. "They are saying something about *what if they find it*? Something about how they should have removed it. Do you think they are talking about Sheila?"

Dagger turned his back to the windows and watched the two men at the conference table. Josh gave the impression he was studying the research papers, but he was leaning close to Flea and whispering. All the while both of them kept glancing at something on the book shelves.

"Take a walk around the back of them and see if you can determine what they are looking at. Maybe there's a switch hidden under one of the shelves that opens up a wall."

Sara watched the two men, how their eyes glanced toward a section of the bookshelves. She slowly made her way behind them while her eyes examined the shelves looking for hinges. Her intense focus on the books appeared to make the two men nervous. She circled the table and moved closer to the shelves as an anomaly caught her attention. As she reached toward one of the shelves, both men slowly rose, eyes wide, mouths gaping.

"Don't..." Flea shrieked, then covered his mouth with his hand.

Dagger moved from the window. "What did you

find, babe?"

"I can't reach the books on that shelf."

"What's so interesting about those? There's a whole wall of books," Josh said, but his hand nervously ran down the back of his hair.

"I, uh, oh god." Flea's fingers clutched at his face.

Dagger tried moving one of the books but it was attached. "They are fake." Dagger pulled off a false group of five books.

"Oh, jeez." Josh grimaced and hung his head.

"It's a recorder of some sort." Dagger brought it down and set it on the table. This got Padre's attention as he abandoned his game of solitaire.

"I think there's another one back there." Sara pointed at a shelf two sections over.

"How the hell could you tell?" Josh said.

Padre studied the two black boxes. "What are these? Spooky voices? Women crying in the night? Woo woo sounds? This what you planned to use on Sheila Monroe to try to get her to write a glowing report on the Indiana Paranormal Investigators?" Padre asked.

"What!? NO!" Josh stammered. "You still think we had something to do with her disappearance?"

"Sounds reasonable to me." Dagger noticed Sara's eyes had returned to normal. "Sheila saw you planting them or discovered them the way Sara did and you panicked."

"There's no way anyone could see them. They were too well hidden." Josh turned to Sara. "How did you see them? My camouflage was flawless."

This produced a huff of air from Venus. "I should

have known you two were up to no good. 'Come join us. We'll get a TV show out of it,' she mimicked. 'We've made fantastic discoveries. We'll be on the cutting edge.' Cutting edge, my foot. What I do is legitimate."

"Huh!" Josh waved her off. "Yours is nothing more than a carnival act."

"What? Why you." Venus made a move around the table but Padre grabbed her arm just as a loud crash of thunder rattled the windows.

"If the crystal ball fits," Josh jeered

"Hey." Dagger waved the faux books in his hand. "Let's get back to this." He held up a three-sided display. Someone had gone to a lot of trouble to gut five hardcover books, gluing them so they stood side-by-side. The back of the book on the left and the front cover of the book on the right completed the three-sided concealment.

Skizzy gave them the evil eye. "Which one of you morons has the controller?"

Josh and Flea locked eyes but neither said anything. Padre held his hand out. "Cough it up. What does your little toy do?"

Josh grimaced and tossed an angry glare at Dagger before jamming a hand in his pocket and pulling out what looked like a remote key. Skizzy ripped it from Josh's hand and pressed a button.

A young girl's voice could be heard. *Julia.*

Skizzy pressed the button again. *Mommy?*

"You frauds!" Venus tried again to make a move toward Josh but Padre lunged and wrapped his arms around her waist. Her right arm swung toward the lanky giant but she missed him by a foot. She tried with her left arm but missed again as Padre held her back.

"Calm down, Venus. You really didn't think ghost hunting was on the up and up, did you?" Padre gently forced her into a chair.

"I can't believe I let you jeopardize the integrity of my craft." A tinge of pink rushed to her cheeks. "My goddess, if this gets out."

"Well, seems like all three of you had something to lose if Miss Monroe had written a negative column about her experience here." Dagger took the remote from Skizzy and studied the mechanism. Anyone with Flea's electronic knowledge could have put this together.

"That's ridiculous. She never knew it was there." Beads of sweat started to form on Josh's forehead.

"Sheila is known for her stealth reporting," Dagger said. "While you were upstairs she would have climbed on a chair and searched every nook and cranny for evidence that you were even the slightest bit deceptive. Believe me, if there was something to find here, she would have found it."

"No, no." Flea was shaking his head back and forth. "We wouldn't have." He paused and looked sharply at Josh. "At least I know I wouldn't have done anything." He stressed the word "I."

"What are you saying?" Josh turned on his friend.

Skizzy took a step back. "FOOD FIGHT."

"Everyone sit down. NOW," Padre yelled.

Josh yanked the chair back and fell into it. "Real nice, Flea. How long have we known each other?"

"You were the one who invited that Lansky guy to join us at that farm house in Demotte and he up and went missing," Flea said.

"Whoa, wait." Padre held his hands out like a traffic cop. "You had someone else who went missing?"

"Oh, dear gods and goddesses." Venus hid her face in her hands.

"He didn't go missing," Josh argued. "The weasel was a college jerk. Thought he'd pull a fast one and plan his own fake ghost but our tape recordings had the ass peeing in his pants. He snuck out and called a buddy to pick him up a mile down the road. Let us think he was missing. The cops found him sunning on the beach by the Planetarium. Rich bastard always loved screwing with me."

"So you lied in your interview." Padre studied the two men with more interest. He despised it when suspects were evasive.

"No, you never asked the right question."

Padre wanted to leap across the table at Josh. He looked over at Dagger who remained leaning against the book shelves. Dagger gave a slight shake of his head indicating that Padre wasn't going to get much more from these two. Eventually something was going to give them away, if they were involved.

"Anything else hidden in this house?" Dagger asked. "Any recorders upstairs?"

"Would you even trust them to tell the truth?" Venus eyed Josh with contempt. Then she took a deep breath. "I have to stop this. Negative vibes are bad for my karma."

She pulled her legs up and sat yoga style, the tops of her hands resting on her knees, thumbs and index fingers touching.

A bright flash of light was followed by another clap of thunder, this time sounding as though it were right overhead. The sky outside was turning a dull and menacing shade of green. The room became silent as candlelight flickered against the walls creating shadowy pockets that darted in and out of the furniture groupings.

"So we have one missing reporter, a guy missing for fourteen months who mysteriously appears, all within a stone's throw from this house, and both of which have something in common." Padre pointed a finger across the table. "You three."

Venus's eyes snapped open. Josh and Flea remained silent. "We're just as baffled as the rest of you," Venus said. "They may be jerks but I was here with them the entire night. We never saw that guy. I can attest to that. As the goddess is my witness."

"Aw, shit. I just lost my super duper battery backup. How can that be?" Skizzy pounded on the monitor.

The wind outside sounded like a freight train headed straight for them. Seven people sat across from each other at the conference table as some unseen breeze made the candle flames flicker. Shadows continued to dance along the walls and appeared to join the shadows in the foyer where more candles flickered on the tables. Something heavy blew against the side of the building near the French doors. Venus gave a "yelp" while Josh nervously drummed the table with his fingers.

"Well," Skizzy started, "if anyone is interested, before I lost power I was checking on the weather history in this area during the previous Rain Man crimes. I think I can summarize it by saying we are screwed."

31 Sheila slowly rose from the couch and tested her legs. All she wanted to do was sleep but the storm wasn't letting up. In all of her years she had never seen a storm so strong or last so long. She stepped into the hallway and stood at the bottom of the stairs. There weren't any sounds coming from upstairs. Between the bursts of thunder she heard muffled voices from outside.

Sheila opened the front door to find Adrian and Colleen on the porch. Adrian sat on one of the rockers. Colleen was standing at the railing, her small hands reaching out to catch rain drops. Puddles of mud surrounded the house like a moat.

"It never lets up." Sheila took a seat and reached around her neck, forgetting that her scarf was missing. "You didn't see a red floral scarf around this house, did you?"

Colleen looked at Adrian and quickly returned her attention to the rain. The young girl seemed to be calm as long as the lightning and thunder had quieted down.

"Did you have a nice nap?" Adrian crossed his legs. He appeared out of place in his suit with long tails and high-collared shirt. Didn't he own any casual clothes?

"Does it ever stop raining?" Sheila asked.

"I love the rain." Adrian leaned back with a sigh. "It brings so many possibilities, or at least it used to. Oh, for the good old days."

"I like rain but I don't like thunderstorms," Colleen said. "It brings death," she added in a voice so quiet Sheila wasn't sure she heard her correctly.

It was the glare Adrian drilled toward Colleen that sent a shiver through Sheila. There had been several previous comments Colleen had made innocently that Adrian didn't like.

A bolt of lightning split in two and darted in opposite directions. This was followed closely by ground-shaking thunder which sent Colleen running to Sheila who wasn't too concerned. It was all a dream and there had been a bad storm when she was at the Sebold mansion. She wondered how the others were faring. Were they still at the mansion? Were they at her bedside? Knowing her father he was probably interrogating them all, wanting to know exactly how she was injured and wondering how much he could sue them for. Maybe she had gone outside during the storm and been hit on the head by flying debris, like Dorothy in *The Wizard of Oz*. That had to be the answer.

"Storms used to be more enjoyable. I was able to come and go as I please."

"What do you mean?" Sheila tried to jog her memory. Had there been something about storms in her research? Maybe there had been a flash flood through Dawson's Corner.

"I used to enjoy moving around in a storm. Few people would be out with all the lightning. Fear can be very intoxicating."

Colleen tugged on Sheila's arm. "I want to go inside now."

"Okay, sweetie." Sheila turned to see Adrian watching the skies. There was a strange smile on his face. He had been too vague about his life history. "Maybe we can continue the interview."

"That would be most enjoyable." He motioned toward the door. "Shall we?"

They congregated in the study. Sheila found it strange that neither Adrian nor Colleen had anything to eat or drink. Matter of fact, she wasn't even hungry. Then again, she can't recall ever eating or drinking anything in her dreams which only supported her theory that she was asleep or in a coma.

Sheila opened the top drawer of the desk and grabbed the notepad and a pen. The pen seemed out of place in this turn of the century dream. "Strange for you to have a pen like this. How did you come across it?"

"It was the man's," Colleen said. She was seated on the floor, one of her dolls in her lap.

"Colleen." Adrian's word of caution had Colleen bowing her head.

"What man?" Sheila's reporter instincts kicked in. Other than the three of them, Sheila hadn't seen anyone else either walking outside or riding.

"A guest who's no longer here," Adrian replied.

"Where did he go? How did he leave? I haven't seen any vehicles much less a road out of this place." Things weren't making sense before and they were making less sense now. She saw Colleen's young eyes jump to Adrian's face. His remained hard to read.

"Not sure where he was headed. He just up and left."

If Sheila didn't know better she'd swear he was trying to erase any hint of a smile on his lips. "Tell me about your childhood." Sheila set pen to paper and waited.

"My childhood. Well, I was a lazy student. Father was embarrassed and vowed to pound some discipline into me. Mother read biblical passages as though God himself was going to come down and transform her ignorant son into a valued scholar. I was thin and sickly, always coming down with something. I swear Doctor Cullerton spent more time in our house than in his clinic."

"Doctor Cullerton. Why does that name ring a bell?" Sheila was sure she came across his name during her research.

"It's a pretty common name." Adrian continued. "Mother had tutors come in to bore me with math and literature and reading. It's a pity I didn't take to reading until I reached thirty years of age. I missed out on a lot of the classics."

"What did your father do for a living? What did your mother do? You don't sound like you liked them very much."

Adrian turned dark eyes on her and without a hint of regret said, "I hated them both. Mother the most."

"And why is that?"

Adrian appeared to stall. Sheila at first thought he was giving it consideration but it was definitely a stall. Maybe he didn't want to talk in front of Colleen who was curling her doll's hair around her finger and paying little attention to their conversation.

Outside the sky remained overcast, as though nighttime never came. But why should it? When you dream you can create whatever weather you wanted. Why Sheila couldn't conjure up sun and white sands was beyond her. Lightning continued its show as it streaked across the sky. Sheila was sure some shrink would find meaning behind this dream and its characters. Colleen moved a little closer to the couch where Sheila sat.

"Mother liked to render her version of spare the rod, spoil the child. Except in her version she liked to tie me to a post in the barn, strip me, and use a horse whip until she drew blood. If I dared to cry out, she would pour salt on the wounds and start all over again."

His face seethed with hatred. Sheila didn't remember either of her parents ever raising a hand to her. Some would say she needed it and she would be the first to admit she was spoiled rotten. But Adrian grew up in another era, one where authorities never questioned what parents did to their children.

"Where was your father during all this?"

"Watching," Adrian replied, dragging the word out with sheer loathing. "The look of utter glee on mother's face was bested by father's" He snapped a quick gaze at Colleen, then lowered his voice and leaned forward slightly. "Perverted pleasure. He was in a state of, how do I delicately put this in mixed company."

"I think I get the picture." Sheila was sickened by even the thought of what some people were capable of. "I find him…both of them, utterly disgusting."

He cocked his head as though sizing up her response. Finding it more than acceptable he said, "Thank you. It is comforting to know I was not alone in my feelings." Adrian cast another gaze toward Colleen, this time exhibiting an unusual display of affection. "There are some things society should never tolerate. Harm to a defenseless child, no matter the age, should be number one." He leaned closer and lowered his voice. Colleen started to hum as she continued to play with the doll's hair. "It was when father turned his attention to Colleen that I knew I had to act."

Sheila's pen hovered. Colleen was such a beautiful child and the thought of a father, or any adult, turning his deviant attention on her was unfathomable. "What did you do?" she asked him.

"I killed them," he said simply. "Both of them. I was sixteen years old."

Sheila stared. Colleen continued to hum. If Adrian had been sixteen and Colleen six, why was Adrian an adult now and Colleen still a child? "But that means you are only ten years older than Colleen yet...how can that be?" She waved her hand as though erasing the confusion. "Forget it. I'm in a coma, it's just a dream. I once dreamed I was a fairy, like Tinker Bell, and flew around the city."

"What's a Tinker Bell?" Colleen asked.

"From the Peter Pan book and movie," Sheila replied. "You know, well, I guess you wouldn't know."

The clouds outside the windows were starting to accumulate, gathering for some planned finale. The rain erupted in torrents, bringing the visibility down to practically nothing. Sheila could barely see past the one tree which crouched outside the window. There was a gleam in Adrian's eyes as he walked closer. He inhaled deeply as though he could smell the rain through the walls.

32 Skizzy paced in front of the windows, bony arms crossed as though keeping himself together. "Wish the storm would just blow over already. It seems to hover over us like we're in some weird snow globe, just this house and the storm." He stopped abruptly and pressed his face closer to the glass. "And will you look at that."

They gathered next to him and waited. As lightning lit up the acreage they could see a mist crawling out of the forest, the warm ground meeting cold rain. It crept and spread, bringing with it a sense of isolation. "Reminds me of that movie, *The Crawling Eye.*"

"Oh, dude. Did you have to mention that?" Flea whined.

"Shhhhh." Sara cocked her head and listened. A hush fell over the room.

Dagger listened intently but didn't hear anything.

"Do you hear that?" Sara took several steps toward the door. "The music box. It's playing." She ran out of the room without even grabbing a candle.

Dagger told Skizzy, "Watch them," as he and Padre chased after Sara. Candlelight bounced off the walls as they took the stairs two at a time. Sara reached the landing and now the two men heard the music, too.

"Shit, I'm gonna have a freakin' heart attack." Padre pressed a hand to his chest. "Slow down." The candle he held had blown out so he took the time to relight it.

Sara slowed her pace, watching for any hint of the same figure she had seen before. She stopped in the doorway and waited for the two men. The waltz continued playing it's tinny tune.

"How the hell did you hear that music box all the way down in the library?" Padre cautiously poked his head around the door jamb. Dagger was the only one who understood how it was possible for Sara to hear what the others couldn't.

They entered the room. The candle Padre held sprayed light against the side wall. The music box sat in the middle of the dresser, the lid propped open. It had been closed the last time they were in the room.

Padre made a sign of the cross. "Okay. Who's got an explanation for this?"

Dagger picked up the music box and checked the bottom. It had a key that had to be wound in order to enable the music box to play. "Maybe we only thought the lid was closed."

"I've heard of music boxes that haven't quite unwound and out of the blue start unwinding again. That's plausible, right?" Padre asked hopefully.

"Maybe. Maybe not." Sara glanced toward the doorway. She had the distinct feeling they weren't alone.

"Come on. Let's get out of here." Dagger ushered her to the hallway. "I don't think we are learning anything from those three. I may have to start beating the truth out of them. Dagger and Padre headed toward the stairs but Sara hung back.

Lightning could easily play tricks on one's eyes, making shadows emerge, dodge, and disappear. But one shadow had substance. Sara watched as it pressed close. She felt her hair being lifted from her back, slowly at first, as though someone had placed a hand under the weight of it all and then sifted the silky strands through unseen fingers. Sara was too shocked to move. Was this another draft as Padre had said or was someone standing next to her? What could possibly hurt her that couldn't be seen? She calmed her breathing, thinking back to one of her grandmother's favorite quotes from Chief Seattle. "There is no death, only a changing of worlds."

"Do you need help?" Sara's voice came out as a whisper.

Something touched her hair and then a voice in her ear whispered. *Stop him.*

"Stop who?" Sara asked. "I need more information."

"Sara?" Dagger and Padre paused halfway down the long hall. Lightning flashed through the windows casting elongated shadows across the hallway, but providing much-needed light.

Sara turned but as her hawk eyes peeled through the darkness, she didn't see anything. Not a mist or a form or any hint that someone had been there. Slowly she joined Dagger at the top of the staircase.

"Did you see your friend again?" A smile tugged at the corners of his lips.

"What?" Padre looked from Dagger to Sara. "What's

he talking about?"

"Someone whispered to me."

Padre laughed. "You're kidding, right?"

"Man or woman?" Dagger asked.

"Man. He said 'stop him.'"

"Hey!" Padre said. "Enough with scaring this old man."

A loud crash of thunder appeared to shake the very floor they were standing on. Padre felt like hanging onto the wall. There wasn't a pause between the crashes. Candle flames bent sideways and were extinguished. Before they had a chance to react, an ear-piercing scream erupted from the bowels of the building and the three were off and running again. Lit candles at the bottom of the staircase were the only things that kept them from stumbling down or losing their footing. In a dark corner of the foyer near the entrance to the library Venus was huddled in a ball, her eyes wide in terror.

Skizzy emerged from the library, a candleholder in each hand. "What's all the hollerin' about? Are you trying to wake the dead?"

Dagger's Kimber was in his hand and now Padre pulled his Glock.

"Holy sheeeiitt." Skizzy held the candles aloft and nodded toward the far wall. Blood was splattered on the white marble floor and across the wall. It looked as though someone had tried to spray paint the wall.

"What the hell?" Padre holstered his gun and held his hands out to keep everyone back. They stood silent, taking the scene in, their eyes assessing each other. Whose blood was it? Was everyone accounted for?

Flea strolled in from the hallway and came up short when he saw everyone standing in the foyer. "What's up?"

"Where the hell were you?" Padre demanded.

"Bathroom. Why?" Flea's eyes slowly registered the carnage. "Holy...oh my god...what happened?" He wrapped his arms around his thin frame, his body turning away from the blood, then rocking back toward it as though his brain were trying to absorb the situation. "Venus?" Flea finally looked down at the young woman and saw the blood on her face. "I...I gotta get outta here."

Padre grabbed Flea's arm. "No one is going anywhere. Now pull yourself together."

"Where's Josh?" Sara asked. She looked to Skizzy who was the last one to emerge from the library. "Was he with you?"

"No." Skizzy nodded toward Venus who had yet to move or even blink. She kept staring at the blood on the floor. "Josh and Venus got into a heated discussion, a continuation of that whole taping thing."

"Josh?" Flea's eyes widened as he ran trembling hands through his hair. "What the hell is going on?"

Padre moved closer to the pools of blood, walking around to the left side. Dagger mirrored his movements on the right side. "This is arterial spray," Padre said. "See how bright red it is? The direction of the spray tells me he was standing near the wall. There isn't any way someone could have walked away with this type of injury. There aren't any footsteps leading away from the blood."

Padre was right. Dagger saw a clean patch of flooring.

He watched as Skizzy and Sara helped Venus to her feet but as she stood the candlelight revealed splashes of blood on the front of her dress.

Padre moved over to Venus and studied the blood, turned her hands over, then her arms. "This isn't her blood. She was facing Josh. Anyone see a knife anywhere?"

"What?!" Flea stammered. "You think Venus stabbed Josh? You can't be serious. Venus wouldn't hurt a fly. Shit, man. What the hell is going on?"

Skizzy searched Flea's clothing for blood, then examined Flea's glazed eyes. He backed away when he detected an odor. "You been drinking, boy? Is that what was in that flask you've been hiding?"

"Nnnno. And what business is it of yours?"

Dagger had enough. He grabbed a fistful of fabric, pulling Flea up on his toes, and jammed the Kimber against Flea's throat. "You have a fourth member lurking around this place, don't you?"

"What? No!" Flea struggled but Dagger's grip was strong. He pressed the gun harder and watched the kid's Adam's apple bob. Dagger took several steps, dragging Flea along, then slammed the sack of skin and bones against the wall.

"Dagger!" Sara wrapped her hands around Dagger's arm. "STOP."

"SILENCE." Padre had to shout over the noise of the storm. How like the chief to be safe and sound at home, probably having his third scotch and water while Padre was stuck in a haunted house with not one, but now two missing people. "God, my head is splitting. Everyone calm down. Dagger, put your gun away. Sara, see if you can get Venus to tell you what the hell happened here."

As though her legs could no longer hold her up, Venus started to buckle, her dress pooling around her. Dagger caught her before she landed in a heap. She stared off seeing nothing, not acknowledging anyone. He waved a hand in front of her face but Venus never flinched.

Sara knelt next to the shaken woman. She clasped her hand and squeezed. Her other hand brushed hair from Venus's face. "Venus, we need your help. We have to find Josh. He might need medical attention. Do you understand? Can you help us?"

"Oh my god," Flea mumbled, rocking back and forth on his feet, turning in half circles, eyes darting as though looking for a quick exit.

Slowly, Venus turned her head toward Sara. Sara smiled with encouragement but the only response were streams of tears. Her body started to tremble. Sara thought she heard Venus try to speak. "Can you repeat that, Venus?"

Padre edged closer as did Skizzy. As Venus spoke her eyes jerked over Sara's shoulder, beyond the staircase and back to the area stained with blood. Her left hand reached out and clutched Dagger's arm. Sara wasn't sure she heard Venus correctly. She looked at Dagger for clarification but then Venus repeated the words, her voice a shaky whisper.

"The wall took him."

33 Sheila had no way of knowing what time of day it was. There wasn't one workable clock in the house. It was dark out, but was it the storm or was it nighttime? She was getting used to the never-ending downpour. As one dark cloud passed, another rumbled in bringing with it lightning and winds that whipped through the property like a tornado.

She crossed the room to the desk and sat down. Maybe if she wrote a time line things would start to make sense. She opened the desk drawer to look for paper. There were several sheets of expensive linen stationery. *Sebold Shipping* was embossed in gold across the top. Why would Adrian have Sebold stationery? But her thoughts were interrupted by another object in the drawer...a wallet. Sheila flipped it open and studied the drivers license. Rick Jensen from Cedar Point, Indiana. The license expired last year. Sheila sat back and studied the photo. Where had she seen him before? Where had she heard the name? She closed the desk drawer, shoved the wallet in the pocket of her slacks, and went in search of Colleen.

She grabbed a candle and made her way upstairs. Sheila found the girl in what looked like a playroom. All of the drapes were drawn so Colleen couldn't see the lightning. She was sitting on the floor surrounded by dolls all dressed in Victorian clothing. Her entire body looked coiled, tense, as though waiting for the next clap of thunder. Sheila pulled the wallet from her pocket and sat on the floor next to the girl.

"Colleen, I found this downstairs. Do you know where your brother got it?"

"What is it?"

"It's a wallet with a drivers license which expired in 2010, Colleen." But Colleen's young eyes showed confusion. How silly to think any of this would mean anything to her. "Do you remember seeing this man? His name is Rick Jensen."

"He came during a storm," she whispered, her eyes searching the doorway.

"Do you know what happened to him?"

"He left during a storm."

"I'm sorry, sweetie. I don't understand." *How could someone from 2011 meet Colleen and her brother? Why not? Since when has anything made sense?* Sheila thought. But Rick Jensen didn't factor into her research, unless. Of course! He must have been a previous news story which was why Sheila was blending research from the early 1900s with current events. "Forget it. My brain isn't making much sense right now. Please don't mention this to your brother. I don't want him to think I was snooping."

"Okay." Colleen cradled the doll in her lap and looked up at Sheila with soulful eyes. She was fearful on one hand but also sad. Where were other young children for her to play with? Did she never leave the house? "Can you stay here?" Colleen asked, whispering as if the walls could hear.

"Sure. But there is a lot more room downstairs in the study. Besides, the couch is more comfortable to sit on than the floor."

"No. I mean can you stay here forever? I don't want to be alone."

Her plea pulled at Sheila's heartstrings. "Oh, sweetie." As though sensing what Sheila would say, tears started welling in Colleen's eyes.

Colleen leaned forward and whispered even lower. "I don't EVER want to be alone."

34 "There is nothing as eerie as complete silence," Skizzy said. And he was right. As though someone had pressed a button, all sounds from the storm had ceased. "I think we are in the eye of the storm." They stood at the bottom of the staircase listening and waiting. They had carried Venus to the library and placed her on a couch. Flea was curled up in a corner chair with his flask, his eyes darting from Venus to dark corners of the room for unseen villains. Skizzy had grabbed the portable scanner, but like everything else, the battery was drained.

Sara heard a faint buzzing that sounded as though it were coming through the walls and floor. A second later all of the lights snapped on. "Power!" Skizzy cheered. He ran back into the library and returned with the power cord for his scanner.

Padre and Dagger moved down the hall and into the adjacent room. According to the blueprints, this was the tea room, a place where the owners entertained visitors with tea and cookies during the day and after dinner drinks in the evening. The wall between the tea room and the extended foyer were five inches thick. Padre knocked on the wall while Dagger pulled to see if it slid open.

Skizzy ran the scanner across the wall. On the monitor

he saw their images. He aimed the scanner as high as the ceiling and then across the entire wall. They were looking for any explanation as to where Josh had gone. "What the hell did Venus mean when she said "the wall took him?"

"Try the floor," Sara suggested. They avoided walking on the blood-splattered portion of the floor. The picture on the monitor showed the usual ghostly image of flooring and piping. The images from the wall yielded little more.

Dagger and Padre returned. "Anything?" Dagger asked.

"This isn't logical." Padre pulled his cell phone out. "Still no service. I can't even get a crime scene crew out here. There aren't any blood drops leading out of this foyer so Josh can't be roaming the house, not with this much blood loss."

Sara walked to the entryway and opened the front door. She stepped out onto the dark veranda. Even the rain had stopped but the sky warned that Nature wasn't done with them yet. A darker shade of black loomed on the horizon slowly circling like a cauldron. She heard footsteps behind her as the three men emerged.

"Look at the driveway," Padre said. Now that the power was back on, it appeared that every light in the mansion was illuminating the surrounding property. What Padre was pointing at wasn't the driveway but beyond. The ground could no longer hold all of the water so the street at the end of the drive looked like a lake. Mist rose from the water like steam, and appeared to travel on wispy feet across the drive. "I don't think anyone will be coming or going out of this place anytime soon. Wonderful. And I left my holy water at home."

"What are you looking for, Sara." Dagger followed her gaze. Several hundred yards to the north they could see several power transformers.

"I'm listening to the power lines," Sara replied.

"Ooooh, I think you just sparked my brain cells, girlie." Skizzy rubbed his hands together. "I've often wondered if there was any truth to the wild stories."

"What the hell are you talking about?" Dagger didn't like the mad scientist look in Skizzy's eyes.

"I'm not sure but whatever I say is going to really sound strange."

Padre chuckled. "I really love hanging with you guys. You are just a laugh a minute. Whatever you say, Skizzy, isn't going to sound as strange as the events of the last three days."

Skizzy's words were cut short as the lights flickered several times and then they heard a series of loud bangs as though every door in the house was being slammed shut, and then the front door slammed in one final angry thrust.

They stood frozen in place, not sure if it was safe to enter. Then as though some spectral apology were being extended, the front door slowly opened and the power was returned.

"That is one pissed off ghost," Skizzy whispered.

Sara shook her head. "Or one desperate one."

"Don't start that shit." Padre slowly pulled his gun. "There is a logical explanation for everything. The storm going from banchee to Bambi created a vacuum which caused all the doors to close. What else could it be?"

"So why the gun, Padre." Dagger brushed past and entered the house. "I for one don't like it when someone messes with my head."

Padre holstered his gun and they cautiously returned to the foyer. "So what can zap all the energy from the batteries and play with the electricity?"

"Ghosts," Skizzy replied. "Exactly what Venus said—ghosts need energy to manifest and they usually draw it from the power source in the room."

"I asked for logic, Skizzy." Padre leaned against the banister and studied the blood platter.

Sara looked past Padre toward the landing and cocked her head. She started up the stairs. "It's the music box again." She ran the rest of the way with Dagger and Padre close behind. The hallways were lit up by the wall sconces and they could see that all of the doors on the second floor were closed. Sara headed for Julia's room, and as she neared the door slowly opened. Padre made a sign of the cross.

Dagger was more suspicious of a human culprit, pulled his gun and held Sara back while he entered first. Immediately he noticed that the oblong bench that had been shoved under the dressing table the last time they were in the room was now tipped over and lying on the floor. It had fallen open and revealed an empty cavity. Sara closed the lid to the music box cutting off the tune. She looked around the room. The only item out of place was the bench.

Dagger holstered his gun, picked up the bench and

studied the interior. "What do you think, Padre? False bottom?"

"Hell, why not? Disappearing bodies, storms from hell, splattered blood. Why not a false bottom?" Padre knocked on the wood but it didn't sound hollow.

"Try the lid," Sara suggested.

The inner lid was lined with fabric which matched the outside cushion. A small gap at the seam was large enough to shove a finger in. He pulled gently, then more forcefully. The lining ripped sending several sheets of paper scattering to the floor.

Padre rifled through the papers while putting them into some type of order. "Looks like some handwritten notes and a police report on Marian Sebold's death. Let's look at all this downstairs. This room gives me the creeps."

35 "So the ghost led you to the hidden papers."
Skizzy appeared to enjoy Padre's nervousness
at the word *ghost*.

"Let's just say there are a lot of things in life one
can't explain." Padre hunched over the police report while
Dagger examined the handwritten notes allegedly written
by Charles Sebold. Sara chose to review the reports the IPI
group had assembled while Skizzy, who finally had power
to his computer, was busy doing Google searches.

"Ahhh, here we go, girlie."

Sara leaned over and studied the computer monitor
while Skizzy jotted down notes.

"What are you two up to?" Dagger asked.

"Never mind," Skizzy said, flicking his wrist. "Just
decipher your own puzzle."

Padre flipped to the second page. "This appears to not
coincide with the official report stated in the newspaper.
The newspaper article said Marian's death was a suicide.
This police report says it was a homicide, that she was
strangled with a scarf." Padre's voice dropped off and they
could barely here the *shit* whispered under his breath.

"Let me guess." Dagger wasn't liking this one damn
bit. "The scarf was tied in a bow."

Skizzy's eyebrows jiggled up and down independent

of each other. "This is getting curiouser and curiouser." He found something he liked on the monitor and jotted down more notes.

"Why would the police not report her death as a homicide?" Sara asked.

"Because," Dagger started, reading from Charles' notes, "the powers that be didn't want rumors of a serial killer running loose in Cedar Point, this coming on the heels of Julia being kidnapped a year before. Sebold hired a private detective to look into other homicides and he discovered that another woman was strangled ten years prior to that, but he wasn't able to dig further."

"Found dead?" Padre asked.

"He was found beaten to death in an alley. Must have been getting close to the truth. Official report claimed it was robbery. Charles Sebold obviously felt all of these cases were connected. Including the kidnapping of his daughter."

"Found it!" Sara claimed as a low rumbling could be heard in the distance. The eye of the storm was moving. "I have been searching through Venus's research hoping to discover what might have been in this location prior to the Sebold mansion."

"You mean like an Indian burial ground?" Padre asked.

"Not quite. Leeland and Louise Walker had a house on this property from the late 1800s until 1918 when the house burned down. Although it was believed the entire family perished in the fire, remains could not be found. According to reports, Leeland was a woodworker but drank more than he built things. Louise was a housewife but according to a local doctor, she was slowly going insane. Doctor Raymond Cullerton felt Louise, Leeland, or both were abusing their son, Adrian. Doctor Cullerton saw signs of aggression in Adrian as early as seven years of age. When Adrian was ten, Louise gave birth to a girl...Colleen. He suspected Adrian of setting the family's house on fire. No one in the Walker family was seen again after the fire but some people claimed to see Leeland, or someone who looked like Leeland, in 1939. A young woman witnessed the murder of a prostitute and described a man who resembled Leeland Walker. That is where it ended."

"If Cullerton saw aggression in Adrian, it would be my guess that the bodies we found in the well were Leeland and Louise. But then how could Leeland have killed someone in 1939?" Padre looked at his companions for answers, but all he received was a strange smirk from the squirrely guy. "Okay, Skizzy. What's with the shit-eaten grin?"

A flash of lightning signaled the start of the next round of storms. Then the clouds opened up. Lightning lit up the gardens revealing a sky churning with fast-approaching clouds. With it came the swirling winds bending the trees and ripping dead branches from their limbs.

"I don't suppose you guys heard of the U.S.S. Victory." After he was met with blank stares, Skizzy continued. "The U.S.S. Victory disappeared in 1918 off the coast of England. It reappeared in the same place it disappeared ten years later. Not one of the sailors on board had aged one day. Now, how can that be, you ask.

"This is where it gets interesting." Skizzy was interrupted by violent flashes of lightning interspersed with pounding thunder while the rain morphed into hail. Skizzy raised his voice to be heard over the storm. "Authorities believe a combination of the magnetic fields and electrical charge brought on by the lightning opened a portal. These two elements combined with the year of a solar storm which has a ten to eleven year cycle, could possibly account for the disappearance of boats and planes over the years, especially in the Bermuda Triangle."

"Are you outta your mind?" Padre looked to Dagger for a plausible explanation. "Are you listening to this?"

Dagger gave Padre a few seconds to think back to some of their previous cases with the Friday the Thirteenth killer who transformed during a full moon and a Friday the thirteenth, and then the Mitch Arnosky case. Mitch had acquired a scientific prototype that could make him invisible.

"But still." Padre washed his hands over his face, wondering how nice it would be to have a simple homicide again. "How can energy and magnetic fields create that much havoc?"

"Look around you." Skizzy pointed at Padre's cell phone. "We have all these unseen energy fields from cell phones, TV remotes, car remotes, GPS, WI-FI, satellite, cable, microwaves, you name it, criss-crossing the atmosphere. Hell, they mentioned recently on the news that the earth's magnetic field somewhere down in Florida went haywire and all the compasses had to be reset. Add to that the solar storms. Every ten to eleven years the sun throws a hissy fit and flips its north and south poles. One well-placed solar flare through either of the earth's two polar regions which are completely open can wipe out everything. And let's not even talk about alien death rays and radio frequencies."

"That's great, Skizzy. You had us at magnetic fields and lost us at death rays," Dagger said.

"Well try this on, boys and girls." Skizzy leaned across the table, his eyes a strange combination of genius and madness. "That electrical power station just west of here was built in 1917. In 1920 we had a solar flare. That could have been the first time a portal appeared here."

Padre sighed, waiting for Dagger or Sara to contradict him but they were silent. "And now you think this Adrian Walker comes and goes every time this portal opens and wreaks havoc then disappears again." Padre tried to choke out a dismissive laugh but it was cut short as a strange green tinge filtered from outside. They could feel the electrical charge in the air as the hairs on their arms bristled. Skizzy quickly turned off his computer as the lights flickered and then died. They each took a collective breath and waited. A deathly howling could be heard as the wind and storm appeared to circle the house. Padre slowly pulled out the crucifix from under his shirt and held it.

Candlelight flickered. A soft whimpering could be heard from a corner of the room. Skizzy let out a chuckle. "I just knew when things started popping the little guy would curl up in a fetal position and suck his thumb."

Sara locked eyes with Dagger across the table,

silently wondering if he gave any credence to Skizzy's assessment. It was one of the most far-fetched ideas she had ever heard from Skizzy. His *big brother* conspiracy theories paled in comparison.

"Is no one going to call his idea crazy?" Padre said. "Are we supposed to believe Sheila has stumbled into some...some..."

"Parallel universe," Skizzy whispered. "Come on, copper. You can say it."

But he couldn't. Padre looked to Dagger for some intelligent explanation but Dagger just shrugged.

"That would explain Rick Jensen," Sara said.

"Absolute...in...tee, girlie. Time stands still in a parallel universe, just like those sailors. You go in at age twenty and fifty years later you are still twenty. How's that for a face lift?"

"But doesn't time eventually catch up with you?" Sara asked. "Don't you suddenly age?" But a movement in the foyer caught her attention. Between the continuous lightning and lit candles in the foyer, there was enough light to determine that something strange was happening. Sara called on her enhanced vision to make sure she wasn't imagining things. She clamped a hand on Skizzy's arm. "Skizzy, the wall," Sara said. "It's rippling, like a mirage in a desert."

"There's the portal." Skizzy rose from the table as Padre and Dagger headed for the doorway. They gathered at the foot of the staircase and watched as a portion of the wall started to reshape itself.

36 Sheila had searched the entire second floor but couldn't find Colleen. The lightning show was non-stop now, but Sheila was so used to the thunder that the vibration in the floors no longer affected her. Where was Adrian? Maybe there was a storm shelter under the house where Colleen and Adrian were hiding. She had witnessed one other tornado in her lifetime and the storm outside was fast approaching tornado level.

Rick Jensen's wallet still bothered her. And it had to be Jensen's cell phone that Adrian possessed. If Rick Jensen had been here, where did he go? Were there others besides Jensen? Was there a way out of this town? She was beginning to doubt that she was in a coma, but what other explanation could there be?

She opened a closet door but found only more suits. Hopefully, Adrian was with Colleen and wouldn't know that Sheila was snooping in his room. The wooden floors squeaked under her weight so she tried tiptoeing across the floor to a book case. On one of the shelves was what looked like a scrapbook. She glanced quickly at the doorway, then set the scrapbook on the desk and flipped through it. Instead of photos there were newspaper articles. There weren't any articles newer than 1949, as though it were the last year a newspaper had been purchased.

As she flipped back to the beginning, a piece of paper flew out and landed on the floor. Sheila picked it up and slowly felt the room spin. It was an obituary for Colleen Walker. At the age of four she had fallen down a flight of stairs and broken her neck. The only witness had been her fourteen-year-old brother, Adrian.

"Find something interesting?" Adrian stood in the doorway, a murderous gleam in his eyes. All Sheila could think of was that beautiful little girl who said her name was Colleen.

"This article says your sister died. Who is the little girl you are holding prisoner?" she demanded.

Adrian smiled. "I do love a feisty woman."

"Answer my question." Sheila wasn't about to be intimidated by the likes of him.

He advanced slowly, exuding an air of confidence. He glanced briefly at the scrapbook and by god she could swear he looked proud. "I was saving my sister from the brutality of my parents. As I was growing older and would be able to defend myself, I knew they would turn their attention to her."

Sheila wasn't buying it. "You were jealous. I bet they doted on her and you couldn't stand it. You pushed her down the stairs, didn't you?"

"Think what you want."

No wonder Adrian was so many years older than Colleen, or whoever the little girl was. Sheila had interviewed cold-blooded killers in prison before and Adrian didn't look much different. If he thought nothing of killing a child, what else was he capable of? And why had he kept this girl alive?

"Why would this little girl be afraid of your mother when she didn't know her?"

"I told her about my mother, even showed her the barn, showed her my scars."

Sheila shuddered at the kind of impression these stories left in a young mind. "You didn't answer my question. Who is the girl and why is she here?"

"She is a companion. As are you."

"Not for long." Sheila threw the scrapbook at him and fled out of the room and down the staircase. She needed to find the little girl and get both of them out of the house. At the bottom of the stairs she started opening doors. Perhaps one led to a basement. But behind one of the doors was someone she hadn't expected. "JOSH?"

Josh was covered in blood from a wound to his neck. He fell forward, the bulk of his weight falling against her. Sheila screamed and pushed him off. He fell to the floor with a thud. She heard Adrian descending the staircase with slow, deliberate steps, as though he knew she wasn't going anywhere. She tore down a hallway, but suddenly realized her mistake. It was a dead end.

"What's happening?" Padre stared in shock as the solid wall became a mist of churning smoke. Not sure what was taking place, all four of them hung back while the house shuddered and the howling wind made it feel as though the huge fortress was being ripped from its foundation.

"There's one way to find out. I'm going in there."

"What?" Sara moved in front of Dagger and shoved him back. "Are you crazy? I know what you're doing. You think that's a way to hide from BettaTec."

That was exactly what Dagger was thinking. How like Sara to read him like a book. Her eyes were more than angry. They were fiery and she was doing her best to hold back the tears.

"Look on the bright side, girlie. In ten years when the portal opens again, he'll be closer to your age."

Sara turned her fiery gaze on Skizzy.

"Hell, I'm going to join him," Skizzy said. "Let the government try to find me in there."

"NO ONE IS GOING ANYWHERE," Padre yelled but hardly anyone paid attention. They were looking at the wall where a mist was seeping from under the baseboard, spreading like fingers, and swirling around their feet. It was as though hot and cold air had separated.

And then there was a muffled noise. At first it sounded like someone yelling from the basement, but there wasn't a basement. Then it sounded like a scream from outside, from somewhere in the forest. The scream intensified until the four realized it was coming from somewhere behind the wall.

Suddenly two figures burst through, as though ejected from the wall, a woman pursued by a man who looked dressed for a turn of the century costume party. They knew immediately that the woman was Sheila Monroe. The man grabbed a handful of her hair, spun her around and pressed a knife to her neck. Dagger and Padre pulled their guns.

"DROP THE KNIFE!" Padre shouted.

Sheila was tossed against the side of the staircase. As though waking from a dream the man took in his surroundings, blinked rapidly and gasped. The knife clattered to the floor but it wasn't because of Padre's order. It was because the man's fingers had started to disintegrate and could no longer grasp.

Then the rest of the body began to rapidly age. The skin became dry and brittle, changing from flesh color to brown then black. The eyes sank into the skull while the lips curled back exposing his teeth. The hair, though long, appeared longer as the skull caved in. Sheila didn't just scream, she shrieked. An endless staccato of sheer terror. The turn of the century clothes collapsed as the body inside of them shriveled, muscle and bones turning to dust. Sheila's knees buckled and she fell on her ass as her hands frantically tried to brush his clothes, bones, and dust off of her. But they clung stubbornly to the fabric and her skin so she ripped and clawed at her own clothes desperately trying to remove any trace of his remains.

Slowly the wall became solid again and outside the winds died down and the rain was reduced to a soft drizzle.

37

Sheila fingered the bands around her wrist as she waited for her father's reaction. All he had done since she explained the entire story was pace around the hospital room mangling an unlit cigar. Anna Monroe sat on the bench in front of the window of the private room dabbing her eyes with a handkerchief mumbling, "My poor baby," as though she already reserved a private wing in an insane asylum for her daughter.

Leyton Monroe finally stopped his pacing, pulled a chair up to the bed and grabbed Sheila's hand. "Sweetheart, I have spent years building a publishing empire. I have the respect of the industry. There are big plans for the future and you are going to be part of it. I can't...WE can't let anything ruin our reputation. If a preposterous story like this gets out, that's it. Everything I have worked for, the legacy I hoped to leave to you, it will be gone. Do you understand?" His voice was low and unusually understanding, probably on orders from his wife that their daughter was in a fragile state.

All Sheila could think of was the beautiful blonde girl kidnapped by Adrian Walker. Sheila counted the bands on her wrist again. She knew she had twenty when she entered the Sebold mansion. Now she had ten. She had given ten to Colleen.

"But Daddy..."

"NO!" Leyton yelled, then raised a fist to his mouth as

though shoving the word back down his throat. He watched Anna wring the hankie as though she wished it were his neck. His tone turned more civil. "Sheila, honey. You heard Chief Wozniak's explanation of what took place. Sergeant Martinez was there. Everything he said sounded..." He struggled to find the right word.

"Sane, Daddy? Is that the word you are looking for?"

"Sweetheart, I wasn't implying anything." He took a deep breath and fought images of a front page story by Sheila describing every lunatic detail of what she had dreamed while in a possible coma. And then another image of a story in the *New York Times* questioning the credibility of his newspaper. He couldn't imagine what his stockholders would think.

"Your mother and I feel it best that you go to that spa in Arizona for a few weeks to rest. Your mother will go with you. She was hospitalized while you were gone, you know. Almost had a nervous breakdown that her little girl was dead." Leyton's voice broke and he fought back the tears. "You have been through a lot, sweetheart. The doctors say you suffered a terrible concussion. Those injuries tend to disorient a patient. You are so lucky to be alive. After a nice long recuperation, I just know you will realize this injury caused you to have some pretty bizarre dreams." He refrained from using the term *hallucinations*.

Sheila didn't have any luck holding back her tears. "Okay, Daddy." She swallowed hard and wondered if she really was losing her mind. She sniffed back the tears and shook her head. "That sounds wonderful, Mom. A little sun, yoga, a massage, and I'll be as good as new."

38 Chief Wozniak had the paper spread out on his desk. It had been two days since Sheila Monroe had been escorted by ambulance to the trauma center with a severe concussion and a laceration to her forehead which had bled profusely. Periodically, he would lift his head and glare at Padre and Dagger seated in front of him drinking coffee.

"It's great you got the story buried on Page 20," Padre said. "Nice aerial shot of the smoldering rubble."

"That was Leyton Monroe's doing. The less he had to show and tell, the happier he was. He's just glad to have his daughter back safe and sound. He didn't care too much for the wild stories she was telling him and he definitely didn't want any other reporter catching wind of it."

"That's why it is good you weren't there," Padre said.

"Plausible deniability." Dagger couldn't believe how easy it had been to fabricate a believable cover. "You were able to sit and listen to her with Leyton and show genuine disbelief."

John folded the newspaper and placed it in his bottom drawer. "Got a whole file drawer with your name on it, Dagger. Although I do need to thank you for giving me a convincing explanation for my press release."

The official police report described a secret panel under

the staircase that hadn't been on any of the blueprints. Sheila had fallen down the stairs, been disoriented, and somehow found her way into this hidden room where she possibly passed out. The police report also stated that Josh McReady's remains had been found in the ruins of the mansion. He had been trapped when lightning struck the house. There had been no mention of a knife wound to Josh's body. Venus had no recollection of what had happened that night and Flea had one terrible hangover. Neither Flea nor Venus wanted to be interviewed.

"I am kinda curious, though." John grabbed the carafe and refilled his coffee cup. "I have seen fires started by lightning before but never have I seen so much destruction. Even the damn porcelain and marble melted. You wouldn't happen to have an explanation for that, would you?" He turned his gaze to Dagger.

"Remember how we told you Skizzy had incinerated the Friday the Thirteenth killer?"

"He used that homemade gizmo of his that spews out napalm or something?"

"He doesn't leave home without it," Dagger replied.

Padre smiled at the thought of one-upping the nosy reporter. "Sheila must have put up a fight when you tried to give her your simple explanation of what transpired."

"Oh, yeah. The reporter in her kept firing off questions, like Rick Jensen's wallet she put in her pocket and the blood on her sweater. She claimed it was Josh's but I reminded her of her head wound. Then she told me how she ripped her clothes off to remove the remains of Adrian Walker to which I told her she ripped off her clothes because she kept seeing spiders crawling all over her. Nice suggestion, by the way," he said to Dagger.

"She hates spiders. It all supports the suspicion that she was hallucinating."

"Her clothes got burned in the fire, I led her to believe, along with whatever she thinks she had in her pocket."

Dagger doubted Sheila would stop digging. "She might read about Jensen in the paper."

"Story is already old news. Even if she looks into it, I'll come up with something."

"Amazing how her forehead didn't start bleeding until she stepped out of that portal. Just like Skizzy said, everything seems to standstill." Padre would never have believed it if he hadn't seen it with his own eyes, even though he wanted to payback John big time for sending him to the mansion.

"Well, Sheila wasn't convinced. Wanted her clothes back to have them tested." John shook his head but couldn't keep from smiling. "For my own curiosity I had them tested in an outside lab. Never know who Sheila could seduce into telling her whatever she wanted to know. The blood was hers but also Josh's."

"I trust you destroyed the clothes," Dagger said.

"Oh yeah. Sheila also kept saying she gave ten of those damn animal bands to this Colleen she met whom she now claims is Julia Sebold." John laughed until tears streamed down his face. "The more she talked, the more ludicrous she sounded." John wiped at his eyes. "You do give us entertaining cases, Dagger."

"Hey, you gave this one to me. I had nothing to do with it."

"What's going to happen with the property?" Padre asked. "We can't let anyone buy the place, can we?"

"That attorney is going to take his losses and run. He doesn't even want to pay to have the rubble removed."

"Good. That will discourage anyone from wanting to buy the property. Lord only knows what will happen in ten years." Padre made a sign of the cross.

39 "Hey." Joe Spagnola placed the vase of roses on the nightstand.

"They're beautiful." Sheila combed her fingers through her hair. She knew she looked a mess but she didn't care. Her eyes were puffy from crying and her head was still pounding from the concussion.

"I'd ask you what the hell you thought you were doing but I'm sure your old man already recited that poem." Joe pulled a chair close to the bed and sat down.

"You've got that right. He's shipping me off to a much-needed vacation. Although when I travel with my mother I don't know how much of a restful vacation that can be."

"Well, you had us all worried."

Sheila leaned back with a sigh. Just when Joe thought she might be drifting off to sleep, Sheila said, "I want a baby, Joe."

Joe just about swallowed his gum. "Are you outta your fuckin' mind? What? Did they open a new boarding school in the Hamptons?"

Sheila forced a laugh at that remark even as the tears squeaked from her eyes. She wasn't aware she had been so transparent. Yes, she and kids didn't exactly go together but she couldn't get Colleen/Julia out of her head. If she had imagined her, exactly whom had she patterned her after? The tour she had given school kids recently didn't have one girl who resembled her.

"Guess I'm going through one of those life-altering moments. Silly me." Sheila didn't bother wiping away the tears.

"You've been through a lot, Sheila. I wouldn't spend time with ghost hunters in the daylight let alone at night with a storm cutting you off from the rest of the world." Joe checked his watch. "Baby, I gotta get to work. Will I see you before you leave town?" He bent down and kissed her on the lips.

"Sure." Sheila watched him leave then turned away from the door. Outside the skies were clear. One would never know that they had just experienced the worst storm in the history of the Midwest.

"About time he left."

Sheila turned and smiled. "Were you waiting around the corner until he left?"

"Sure." Dagger took the seat that Joe had vacated. "Not enough space in this room for both of our egos." He had never seen Sheila without makeup before. Even when they were dating she always went to bed with makeup on. "How are you feeling?"

"Other than a pounding headache, physically I'm fine. Mentally, Daddy is sending me to a spa for a few weeks to get these hallucinations out of my system." She slipped a fingertip under the bands on her wrist. "Everything seemed so real, Dagger. All the time I was missing I thought I was in a coma. It seemed all the details from the research I did on Dawson's Corner, Cedar Point and the Sebold mansion took center stage in my mind. Then Daddy says I lost some of the bands, that I didn't give them to some mysterious girl. How could I be missing the exact number that I gave her? It makes no sense."

Dagger had seen a photo of Julia Sebold. If Sheila were ever to have kids, he would imagine her daughter would look just like Julia. He studied the bandage on her forehead. "How many stitches did you need?"

"Twelve. Now I'll have to find a plastic surgeon. Can't have a scar on a perfect Monet." She laughed but the tears fell and she turned serious. "You came to my rescue, Dagger. I knew you would."

"Don't thank me. I didn't want to be involved but it was Sara who convinced me. Besides, your father paid me a hundred grand. Can't pass up that kind of money."

Sheila smiled, it was a sad smile of love lost. Her wedding dress was still hanging in her closet. She had never given up hope that Dagger would come to his senses and realize that Sheila was the only woman for him. "I knew the minute Sara walked into your office that day that she would be the one."

"The one what?"

"Don't give me that, *I'm like a big brother to her. I don't mix business with pleasure* crap. The look on your face that day reminded me of the look my daddy had when he saw his first Mercedes on a showroom floor."

Dagger sighed. He was getting tired of having to constantly justify his relationship with his partner. "She and I are strictly business. You and I fell in lust, not love. To have a physical relationship which involves love just doesn't work for me. Doesn't pay to get emotionally involved. Makes it easier to pick up and move any time I want."

Sheila shook her head, surprised she had to draw Dagger a picture. "You are either really naive or just plain stupid. Face it, Dagger. You can't leave her now."

40 Dagger hung his keys on the key rack and tossed his jacket on a kitchen chair. The house couldn't feel more like home than if he had built it with his own two hands. Although he had always said he trusted very few people, the truth was all of them lived in Cedar Point. This city was the longest he had lived anywhere. The kitchen smelled of popcorn smothered in butter and he could almost feel his mouth salivating. He pulled a beer from the fridge and walked into the living room. The door to the aviary was closed. Einstein was probably sulking because they had left him alone during the storm. Sara was sitting on the couch, feet braced on the coffee table, a bowl of popcorn in her lap. Venus was still in shock, Flea was sucking his thumb somewhere, Sheila was recuperating in a hospital, and here was Sara eating popcorn and watching television.

"How is Sheila doing?"

"Still in denial but slowly accepting the fact that she was hallucinating."

"Do you think Sheila will ever try to spin her story again?"

"Nah. It's her word against the four of us." Dagger studied her, imagining what Sheila had seen when all hell was breaking loose at the mansion. Nothing appeared to affect Sara. It was another day at the office. Sure, the Friday the Thirteenth killer unnerved her because she had never met another shapeshifter. She had needed time afterward to seek answers from an elder back on the reservation where she grew up. If anything, Sara grew stronger, wiser, with every weird case she encountered.

"Einstein's mad. Won't eat or even come out of his tree."

"It will do him good to stew awhile. You spoil him rotten." He sat down and waved a check at her. "Monroe made good on the reward." He tossed the check on the coffee table. Outside the French doors he could see a flame burning in the fire pit in the middle of the yard.

"What do you think will happen with the property? Anyone could stumble into that portal. Skizzy says it doesn't have to be a wall. Just like ships and planes just sailed right through the portal."

"Chief Wozniak talked to Attorney Godfrey. He didn't tell him the truth as we know it. Just about the fire and how the property should be demolished, condemned, whatever. He's getting a fat check from the insurance company so he could care less if the entire forest grows over it."

Dagger's gaze drifted to the yard again. "What are you burning out there?"

"Remember what we promised each other when I returned from my two-month sabbatical after the Friday the Thirteenth case?"

Dagger remembered all too well how angry he was that Sara had left without word and returned without warning. They had each promised to never leave. His eyes drifted to the fire, and the thought of what was burning hit him. "You're burning my suitcase?"

Sara just shrugged. She figured the only reason Dagger kept making threats of a new start and leaving town was because he was waiting for someone to make up his mind for him. She held up the bowl. "Popcorn?"

Dagger felt a strange weight lifted from his shoulders. He should be angry, but he had to admit that Sheila was right. Sara was the one person he could never walk away from.

He watched the images on the wide screen television. Two figures were creeping through what looked like a prison. There were long hallways of cell doors and metal cots. The characters were illuminated by a weird camera light which made their eyes appear to glow.

"What the hell are you watching?"

Sara slowly smiled as she grabbed a handful of popcorn. *"Ghost Hunters."*

EPILOGUE

Puffs of smoke still drifted from the ruins of the Sebold mansion. Charred beams broke and crumbled against what was left of the brick fireplaces. Couches, chairs, and tables were nothing more than burnt remnants of an era gone by. Walls were no longer standing, leaving just a hint of the size of the structure that had once been a part of history. The grandfather clock was charred black, the face non-existent. The two terraces now covered the dried and forgotten garden, crushing the bench where Marian and Julia had sat to have their picture painted by Charles.

The gargoyles stood watch but from a distance, having tumbled from their perches and fallen into puddles of water surrounding the house. A melted face and charred cloth were all that remained of the doll that had been on Julia's bed. Birds had avoided this area, the heat had been so intense. Even now they observed from the safety of the surrounding forest, waiting to see if there was anything worth picking at once the embers died down.

A beam cracked and settled spilling onto the ground a square box that had been spared somehow from any damage. The lid popped open and the music box started playing a waltz.

The tune carried on the breeze as dried leaves scattered across the ground. They leaped and twirled to the tune, tumbling toward the outskirts of the property. At the edge of the forest hidden by brush was a small skeleton dressed in a pinafore and wearing patent leather shoes. Her hair was long and blonde. The earth was slowly accepting the delicate bones and the fabric was disintegrating as though decades old. What wasn't affected by the era were the ten animal bands in various colors that she wore around her wrist.

www.ingramcontent.com/pod-product-compliance
Lightning Source LLC
Chambersburg PA
CBHW061613100726
47898CB00002B/644